語りつぐナガサキ

原爆投下から70年の夏

創価学会長崎平和委員会 編

第三文明社

1945年（昭和20年）8月9日午前11時02分、長崎市に史上2番目の原子爆弾が投下された
At 11:02 a.m., August 9, 1945, the world's second atomic bomb used against human beings exploded over Nagasaki.

爆心地近くの城山小学校の校門に立つ少年平和像
Boy's Peace Statue standing at the main gate into Shiroyama Elementary School near the hypocenter.

語りつぐナガサキ――原爆投下から70年の夏

発刊にあたって

今夏、長崎に原爆が投下され、七十年の節目を迎える。

昨年、被爆者の平均年齢が八十歳に迫り、「被爆者健康手帳」を交付された方が、全国で二十万人を下回った、との報道を耳にした。いまや、戦後生まれが、国民の八〇％を占める時代となった。必然的に、戦争や原爆の記憶が風化し、その継承が叫ばれて久しい。

私は、被爆二世として生まれた。四十年前、私が高校生のとき、友人に呼び掛け、「長崎原爆を語り継ぐ会」を結成した。当時、被爆から三十年を迎えたことを契機に、被爆の実相を聞き、被爆者の叫びを多くの人に届

けたい、と一軒、一軒、歩いて回った。しかし、それは想像以上に困難の連続だった。

被爆者の口は重い。被爆の証言をするということは、封印したい記憶を呼び起こすことにほかならない。それは、凄惨な現場を思い出すだけでなく、鼻の奥にこびりついた〝死の臭い〟の記憶も甦ってくるという。それでも、こちらの思いを伝え続ける中で、証言してくださる被爆者の方もおられた。

そのなかで、忘れられない言葉がある。「あなたたちが若いから、伝える必要があると思う。こんな思いは、もう誰にも味わってほしくないから」。噛み締めるように語られた一言、一言が、衝撃となって、私の胸を貫いた。憎しみや嘆きでなく、被爆者の「他者を思いやる心」に心が激しく揺さぶられた。ここに、被爆証言を後世に継承していく目的があると確信した。

とりわけ、両親や祖父母から、被爆体験を初めて聞いたメンバーも多く、

その鮮烈な内容に打ちのめされそうになった人もいた。一番、身近な家族だからこそ、語らなかった、いや、語れなかったのだと感じた。普段は、見ることも感じることもできない表情に、深い悲しみを感じ、言いしれぬ怒りを覚えたことも事実である。

私たちが聞き取りした証言を収録した「ナガサキを語り継ぐ～高校生による平和の叫び」（一九七六年八月、第三文明社刊）の証言者もいまでは、多くの方が故人となっている。今回の被爆証言集に収録した被爆者の方々のなかには、入市（にゅうし）被爆や胎内被爆、在日韓国人など、それぞれ境遇は異なるが、皆、「これが最後になるかもしれません」と言われ、貴重な体験を語っていただいた。

戦後七十年、被爆七十年は、単なる節目で終わらせてはいけない。節目は一過性でなく、被爆者の叫びを継承しゆく人を広げていく水かさを増していかねばならない。いま、世界を見渡せば、約一万六千発もの核弾頭が

実在する。その一発たりとも、使用させてはいけない。核兵器と人類は、絶対に共存できないのだ。創価学会の戸田第二代会長が叫ばれた「核兵器は絶対悪」との思想を世界精神に高めていくことが、私たち長崎平和委員会の使命である。

今回、被爆証言を日本語と英訳で、発刊することとなった。"被爆者の肉声"を世界に発信する格好の機会となった。この証言集の発刊を通し、"ナガサキの心"を後世に過たず伝えていく、使命と責任を皆さまと共に分かち合うことができたら、幸甚の極みである。

二〇一五年四月

長崎平和委員会委員長　吉岡輝彦

目次　語りつぐナガサキ──原爆投下から70年の夏

発刊にあたって ……… 3

長崎被爆地図：証言者の被爆地点 ……… 12

国連に六万六千人余の核廃絶署名を届ける　　吉田　勲 ……… 14

被爆がもたらした病との戦いは今も続いている　　岩永良子 ……… 30

父母と弟、三人の妹は広島で被爆、三日後に祖母と私は長崎で被爆　　梅林二也 ……… 46

「原爆が伝染る」とひどい差別を受ける	中尾安子 …… 60
祈りを込めて「原爆死没者名簿」を筆耕	谷川正潤 …… 76
「被爆語り継ぎの本つくる」と娘に言われ、長い沈黙を破る	高比良信治 …… 88
被爆を夫に隠し続け、思い悩んだ新婚時代	濱百合代 …… 102
原爆は女性にむごい。生命を宿す「母」を執拗にいじめ続ける	岩本光子 …… 116
「入市被爆」を知らず、被爆直後に爆心地に	福下フサエ …… 132
城山国民学校千五百人の児童が百人に	森本正記 …… 144

苦しさも悲しさも和歌に託して耐えた母　田﨑弥寿子 …… 156

母の遺骨もなく、亡くなったとは信じられない　山口テル子 …… 170

被爆死した同胞たちへの祈りをこめ、チマチョゴリで平和式典に参列　権　舜琴 …… 182

十七歳で特攻隊員となり、「死」を覚悟していた　馬場　博 …… 196

被爆証言を読んで①　山下俊一（長崎大学副学長） …… 210

被爆証言を読んで②　朝長万左男（長崎原爆病院名誉院長） …… 214

口絵写真　©Bettmann/CORBIS/amanaimages（原子雲）
　　　　　©Cogawa/PIXTA（ピクスタ）（少年平和像）

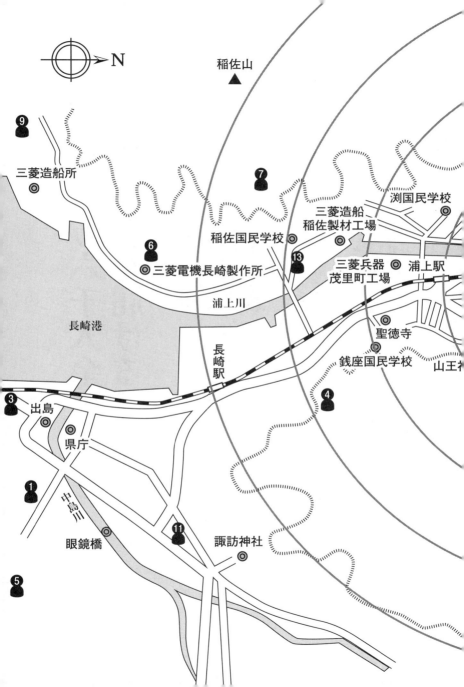

国連に六万六千人余の核廃絶署名を届ける

吉田 勲 さん

よしだ・いさお 一九四〇年(昭和十五年)八月生まれ。爆心地から三・九キロの中新町の自宅で四歳のときに被爆。中学卒業後、さまざまな飲食店で修業し、中華料理店を開く。結婚し、一男三女の父となった後も被爆したことは誰にも話さなかったが、「原水爆禁止宣言」を読んだことがきっかけで、「黙っていてはいけない。声を上げなければ!」と決意。被爆者団体に入り核兵器廃絶の運動に取り組んでいる。七十四歳。長崎市古賀町在住。

人生の転機となった「原水爆禁止宣言」

吉田勲さんは、瀬戸物店を営む両親のもとに次男として生まれた。父は早くに亡くなり、吉田さんが二歳のときに兄も病気で亡くなり、当時、まだ二十代半ばだった母は、祖母の勧めもあって、その年の暮れに再婚した。吉田さんは祖母に引き取られ、祖母と二人だけの暮らしが始まった。それから三年が経(た)ち、吉田さんはあと十五日で五歳を迎えようとしていた。

あの日、私は爆心地から三・九キロ離れたオランダ坂近くの中新町の自宅にいました。
祖母は共同井戸で洗濯をしていましたが、その横で遊んでいた私に突然、大きな声で、

「敵機が飛びよるけん！　家ん中に入らんね！」
と、叫びました。
　急いで家の裏口に駆け込みながら、一瞬、空を見上げると、アメリカの飛行機がキラッと光って見えたことを覚えています。
　祖母が洗濯物を持って裏口から家に入ろうとしたとき、窓の外がパーッと明るくなりました。爆音のようなものは聞こえませんでしたが、強い風で障子がガタガタ鳴っていました。
　私はしばらくじっとしていました。ふと、自分の机が気になり二階に上がってみると、そこは窓ガラスが粉々に割れていて箪笥や本箱が倒れ、まるで火鉢でもひっくり返したように、もうもうと煙が舞っているのです。
　呆然としている私に、
「防空壕へ逃げよう」
と、祖母が言いました。

祖母に手を引かれて外へ出ると、曇っていた空でしたが夕方のように薄暗いのです。原子雲が空を覆っていたので太陽が遮られていたということを、私は後になって知りました。

薄暗いなか、家から三十〜四十メートル先の山の中腹にある防空壕へ向かう途中、喉が渇いて仕方がありません。

「水が飲みたい！　水を飲ませて！」

と、私が言っていると、通りかかった兵隊さんが自分の水筒を渡してくれました。その水のおいしかったことを、いまもはっきり覚えています。

崩れた家や、瓦礫（がれき）をかき分けるように歩いていると、一軒の倒壊した家の屋根からトタン板がいまにも落ちそうにブラブラしているのが見えました。それが突然、私のほうへガシャガシャと落ちてきたのです。直撃はしなかったものの、トタン板の端が私の口元に当たり二・五センチほど切れ、血がダラダラと流れ出ました。

17　吉田　勲

祖母が、被っていた手拭いを渡してくれたので傷口に押し当て、「痛いよ！ 痛いよ！」と泣きながら、やっとのことで防空壕にたどり着きました。そのときの傷は、いまも残っています。

防空壕の入り口で振り返ると、駅の辺りが真っ赤に燃えていました。その火はみるみる広がって、翌日には町の三分の一を焼いていたのです。

防空壕の中にはたくさんの人がいて足の踏み場もなく、ムッとした汗や火傷（やけど）の傷口からの臭いで、私は気持ちが悪くなりました。

そこに次々と上半身裸の人や、体じゅう焼け爛（ただ）れた人たちが戸板に乗せられて運び込まれてきます。赤く爛れたところに輪切りのキュウリが貼られていたのを記憶しています。当時はキュウリを貼ることくらいしか、火傷の応急処置はなかったのです。

ひと晩、防空壕にいて、翌日自宅に戻りました。自宅も近所の家も焼けなかったので、そのまま祖母と暮らし、一年半後に仁田（にた）小学校に入学しま

18

した。

ところが、吉田さんが小学校に入学して間もなく祖母が体調を崩したため、翌年、愛知県蒲郡市の父の長姉の家に引き取られることになった。吉田さんは小学校二年から中学二年まで、ここで生活した。伯母夫婦は子どもがなく可愛がられたが、知らない土地ということもあり、吉田さんは「とうとう一人ぼっちだ。自分がしっかりしなければいかん！」という思いを強くしたという。

一般に、原爆症といわれる「放射線の影響による病気」は、十一疾病として指定されていますが、そのうち私に当てはまるのが二つあります。
一つは、腰が徐々に悪化する変形性脊椎症というもので、これは年を経て痛切に感じています。

もう一つは、白血球が減少するもので、私の症状としては体じゅうにかさぶたができるのです。頭、顔、胸、背中と、ところ構わず吹き出物ができ、化膿してジュクジュクになり、やがてかさぶたになるのですが、その痛痒さといったら、気が狂いそうでした。そのうえ、長崎でも転校先の学校でも、「かさぶた野郎！」といじめられたのです。

そんなことも原因となって、私は被爆のことは封印することにしました。「しゃべらない」「話さない」ということではなく、「私とは関係ない」と決めたのです。

「無関係」にすると、八月九日の式典のテレビ報道も新聞記事を目にしても抵抗はありません。我慢しているのではなく、「無関係」なのですから。

これは、小学二年から中学二年まで、愛知県の伯母に引き取られて長崎に住んでいなかったことも原因だと思います。「この六年間で、私の〝被爆〟はすっかり〝薄められた〟のだ」と、勝手に思い込むことにしたのです。

伯母のところでは、飴だったか団子だったか忘れましたが、私は甘い物が欲しくて養父の財布からお金をくすねて買い食いしたことがありました。養父は私がくすねたのに気がついていながら、何も言いませんでした。それがかえって辛く、それからは「欲しいものは自分で働いて買おう」と決め、中学校一年生から新聞配達を始めました。初めての給金で、欲しかった長靴を買ったときはとても嬉しかったものです。

中学三年を目前に、養父が定年となり生活が苦しくなったため、吉田さんは長崎県端島（軍艦島）で暮らす父の次姉の家に引き取られた。ここは三菱造船の炭鉱町で、終戦の復興景気で活気に満ちていた。その頃では珍しい高層住宅の七階が住まいだった。

最後の中学生活を軍艦島で終え、吉田さんは長崎市内のパン屋に住み込みで就職した。

ところが、勤めて三カ月後、パン生地を入れて一つひとつ、パンの大きさに切断する機械を操作していた吉田さんは、生地を押し込んだ拍子に指まで入ってしまい、左手の人差し指切断という大怪我をしてしまう。

しばらく製菓部門に替わったが、祖母から父は亡くなる寸前まで喫茶店を開きたがっていたことを聞き、吉田さんは自分もやってみたくなったという。

そして、梅月堂という喫茶店に勤めたが、「やる以上は本格的に」と上京。高島屋のコーヒースタンドを皮切りに、東京で三年間、コーヒー修業をした。祖母と「三年経ったら戻るという約束」を守り、長崎に戻ったが職はなく、屋台のラーメン屋などいくつかの仕事を経て中国料理店に勤め、今度はコックの修業をした。その後、独立。

独立を機に、結婚相手として、親類からある女性を紹介された。中華料理店を始めたばかりで忙しかったが、当時、佐世保にいた彼女のところに

バイクで会いに行き、駅前の喫茶店で話をした。三度目に会ったのは島原の彼女の実家での結婚式だった。被爆とは「無関係」と決めていたので、吉田さんは妻となった彼女にも、被爆のこととは話さなかった。

忘れもしません。妻が長男を出産するとなったとき、突然、不安が頭をもたげてきたのです。

被爆したことは自覚していたので、「もし奇形児が生まれたらどうしよう」と思いました。妻にも被爆のことは話していないので、不安はつのり、眠れない日が続きました。

当日、私は産院の分娩室扉の前で、「五体満足な子で生まれてきてほしい」と祈りました。

そして、幸い健康に生まれてくれてホッとしました。それから、「何か

あったときのために」と、被爆者手帳を申請したのです。

一男三女の子どもに恵まれ、幸せでしたが、「被爆のことを公にすることだけはやめよう」との気持ちは変わりませんでした。

五十三歳のとき、長女が結婚しました。式を挙げた文化会館二階の壁に、畳一枚分の「原水爆禁止宣言」の全文が掲載されていました。何げなく見ていると、「原爆を使用する者は悪魔であり、魔物であり、サタンである」という趣旨の文面に釘付けになったのです。気がつくと、手帳にその全文を写し取っていました。

最後の方で、「この思想を、この考え方を青年男女は全世界に広めてほしい」と結ばれています。この「青年男女」を「被爆者」と置き換えたら?

五歳から四十八年間封印してきた「被爆」への思いが、一気に突き上げてきた瞬間でした。「黙っていてはいけない。声を上げなければ!」と、

心から思ったのです。

家に戻るなり市役所に電話をかけ、長崎市内に四つあるという被爆者団体の電話番号を教えてもらい、片っ端から電話をかけました。そのなかで、「長崎原爆被災者協議会」の山田事務局長の対応がとても良かったので、「会員になりたい」と申し込んだのです。

さっそく、その週の日曜日に平和公園で行われた「核実験に抗議する市民の会」主催の座り込みデモに、私は初めて参加しました。

それからもこのような活動を続け、二〇一三年の「北朝鮮の三回目の地下核実験に抗議する座り込みデモ」は、私が参加した四十三回目の座り込みデモとなります。

家族に隠すつもりはありませんでしたが、あえて宣言するほどのことでもないと思い、黙っていました。

25　吉田　勲

何回目かの座り込みデモのとき、その様子がテレビで放映されたのです。妻が観ていて、
「あら、お父さんが映っとるやない！　なんで？」
それで四人の子どもたちにも知られてしまいました。知られた以上、子どもたちにも被爆二世として活動をしてほしいと思うのですが、どの子も私ほどの関心はなさそうです。あとは、孫たちに期待しています。
「四十八年間の空白！　その間、被爆に背を向けてきた」という気持ちは、「この空白を取り戻さなくては」という、焦りにも似た気持ちとなりました。

そして、座り込みデモで一緒になった人から、
「こんど東京で、核保有国の大使館に核実験反対の要望書を届けに行くんだけど、行かない？」と、誘われると、
「ぜひ連れて行ってください」と、二つ返事で参加することにしたのです。

26

アメリカ大使館、ロシア大使館、外務省などに核実験反対の要望書を持って何度も上京しました。

また、長崎では「核兵器廃絶運動」の一つとして毎年、「高校生平和大使」を選び、国連本部に核廃絶の声明文を届けています。

「吉田さん、国連本部に行きませんか？」と声がかかり、一九九九年十一月十五日には私が団長となり、三人の高校生平和大使とニューヨークの国連本部でジャヤンタ・ダナパラ事務次長に「核兵器廃絶への署名用紙六万六千四十八人分」を手渡しました。次長は「皆様方の行動を高く評価します」と真摯な態度で話されました。

現在は、スイスのジュネーブにある国連欧州本部に届けています。

その後、二〇〇五年、〇八年、一〇年と計四回、ニューヨークの国連本部を訪問し、〇五年のNPT（核拡散防止条約）再検討会議の傍聴後、ニューヨークのNGOの方々との交流で、

27　吉田　勲

「私たちはヒロシマ、ナガサキのことはあまり知らないのです。もっともっと被爆者の声を直接聞きたいし、聞かせてほしい」
と、話されていたことは強く印象に残っています。

そのときの、五月五日。オハイオ州デイトンの「アメリカ空軍博物館」を見学しました。長崎に原子爆弾を投下したB29爆撃機「ボックスカー号」がピカピカに磨かれて展示されていました。「こいつが原爆を投下したのか！　それで多くの死傷者が出たんじゃないか！」と私は何とも言えない気持ちになり、怒りで体が震えました。

一二年八月九日の長崎平和祈念式典では、原爆投下を指示した当時のトルーマン米国大統領のお孫さんで核廃絶運動を推進されているクリフトン・トルーマン・ダニエル氏が出席されました。

偶然に私もお会いし、核廃絶について誓い合い、悲惨な過去を乗り越える〝歴史的な握手〟も忘れられない思い出となりました。

これからも、被爆を体験した者として、自分の人生の転機となった「原水爆禁止宣言」に込められた「人間主義・絶対平和主義」の思想を胸に、力の限り核廃絶への運動を続けていきたいと決意しております。

被爆がもたらした病との戦いは今も続いている

岩永良子 さん

いわなが・りょうこ　一九二八年（昭和三年）五月生まれ。爆心地から一・一キロの文教町で十七歳のときに被爆し、大怪我を負う。瀕死の状態から回復し、実家で静養する。その後、病院での看護の手伝い、郵便局勤めを経て、結婚。今も被爆が原因とみられる体調不良と戦っている。八十六歳。長崎県西彼杵郡長与町在住。

無数のガラスが全身に刺さり地獄のような痛さだった

県立長崎高等女学校卒業後、特設専攻科生だった岩永良子さんは「報国隊」として、文教町にある三菱兵器製作工場の第二工作部企画課という部署で、兵器の部品製造の事務作業をしていた。業務内容は、部品別に製造にかかった時間を記入するというものだ。事務所は、大きな工場の一角にあった。

自宅は爆心地から十二キロ離れた、深堀にあった。岩永さんは自宅を朝早く出て、六時の船で一時間かけて大波止に着き、そこから市電で通勤していた。

朝八時半頃に職場に着くと、間もなく空襲警報が鳴り、職場の仲間とすぐに裏の山へ逃げた。その後、警報は解除され、岩永さんは工場に戻った

のだった。

 工場に戻り、再び仕事をしていると突然、飛行機の爆音が聞こえました。
「あ、また空襲！」
と叫んだ瞬間、もの凄い閃光とともに爆風が襲ったのです。山は一瞬にして、はげ山になったのですから。山にとどまっていたら即死でした。あのまま、
 閃光と同時に、私はとっさに工場のコンクリートの床にうつ伏せになりました。
 その後のことは、ほとんど覚えていません。記憶にあるのは、「山口さん（旧姓）！」と言って起こしてくれた先輩事務員の植田さんの顔が目の前にあったことです。植田さんとは、その一カ月後に、新興善国民学校の救護所で偶然再会しましたが、顔も身体も怪我をしていなかったのに、一

週間後に亡くなったと聞きました。

そのときの私は、爆風で飛んできたガラスの破片が顔、腕、背中と全身に突き刺さり、血まみれでした。とっさにうつ伏せになったので、お腹は守ることができましたが、工場の天窓のガラスが落下してきて、背中、両腕、とくに右肘はガラスが刺さってザクロのように裂けていたのです。

私の隣で同じように記帳していた事務員さんは、吹き飛ばされてきた窓枠が背中に刺さったまま亡くなっていたそうです。

私は、「逃げなければ！」と、工場の裏口から表に出ました。爆心地側の正面玄関から逃げた人は、その後、二次被爆で大変だったと聞きました。裏口は、すぐに田んぼになっていました。逃げる途中で草履の片方が脱げて、田んぼの泥の中に落ちてしまいましたが、私はそのまま逃げ続けました。

まだ煙の上がっている、熱く焼けた瓦礫の中を歩いていると同級生の西

岩永良子

さんと会いました。西さんは、途中で落ちていた靴を見つけて履(は)かせてくれました。それは子どもの靴で、私の足の半分しかありませんでしたが、とにかく、それをつっかけて逃げました。

西さんは、どこも傷を負っていないように見えましたが、途中、何度も座り込み、げえげえと吐いていました。逃げることだけで精いっぱいで、周りの様子はほとんど覚えていません。

ただ、
「眠るな！」
「水を飲むな！」
と、叫んでいる人がいたことだけは覚えています。

途中から西さんは、元気な男子学生に背負われて避難。背中と両腕にガラスの刺さった岩永さんは、両腕でつかまれないので背負われることがで

きなかった。
民家の婦人が岩永さんの付けている「報国隊」の腕章を見て、県立高等女学校に知らせてくれたため、すぐに先生二人がリヤカーを引いて迎えに来てくれた。リヤカーを見て五人ぐらいの生徒たちが「先生〜」と言って寄ってきました。そして一緒に学校へ向かいました。
岩永さんの足は無傷だったので、ガラスが刺さった部分に気をつけながら、リヤカーに敷いたゴザの上に正座の姿勢で乗っていました。
学校近くで、やはり逃げてきた五人くらいの生徒たちと一緒に、教室に入った。お茶やお花を習うときの畳敷きの「お作法室」に集まり、その夜は、ひとかたまりになって過ごした。時折、B29の爆音が聞こえてくると身をすくめ、おびえた。
みんなは倒れるように横になったが、岩永さんはガラスが刺さっているため横になって寝られない。一晩中、正座したり足を伸ばしたりして夜明

岩永良子

けを待った。

　翌朝、出血がひどいので近くの小学校の救護所に「応急処置だけでも」と、先生が連れて行ってくれましたが、そこへ着くとギョッとしました。皮膚が焼け爛れた、裸同然の人たちでいっぱいなのです。「私の怪我はまだ良かほうたい」と思うと、逆に元気が出ました。そして、順番が回ってきそうもないので、私は再び学校に戻りました。

　その頃、深堀の自宅では「広島に落ちた新型爆弾と同じ爆弾で長崎は全滅」との情報が入り、「爆弾で良子はやられた！」と、家族は泣いていた。

　翌日、学校に収容者の名前が貼り出され、それを見た近所の人が両親に連絡してくれた。

　消防団の父と警察官の叔父が担架を持って迎えに来て、担架に乗せられ

たまま、岩永さんは船に乗り、十日の夜、深堀の自宅に戻った。瀕死の状態で口も利けず、かろうじて意識があるという状態だった。

再び空襲があるかもしれない。その恐怖から、私たちは防空壕に避難していました。壕の中ではむしろを敷いて、その上で休みました。瀕死状態の私を、一番下の妹（当時九歳）が付きっ切りで看病してくれました。

髪は鳥の巣のようにボサボサになっており、細かいガラスが突き刺さってキラキラと光っています。細かなガラス片は、頭や顔にも無数に突き刺さっていました。刺さった傷跡は、数えられるものだけでも三十八カ所もあり、流れ出る血で制服もガバガバになり、身体に張り付いた布地を傷口から剥がす痛さといったら、生皮を剥がされるような激しさでした。そんな私を気遣うように、妹が慎重にハサミで切って剥がし

てくれました。
　背中には、大きなガラスでナイフのようにえぐられた十五センチぐらいの傷があり、骨まで見えていたそうです。
　ガラス片は妹に丁寧に抜いてもらったのですが、身体に入ったガラスの破片は溶けないのでいつまでも残っていて、しばらくすると痛み出します。
　そのたびに、せっかく塞がった傷口を病院で切って取り出してもらうのです。出てくるのは小豆の半分ほどの小さな破片。そんな破片を七個も取り出しました。七十年経ったいまでも、膝の辺りがチクチク、ゴロゴロしているのです。
　何より辛かったのは、仰向けに寝られないことと、両肘から血が流れ出るので両腕を吊ったままでいなくてはいけないことでした。傷の少ない左側に布団を重ね、それに身体を預けるようにして両腕を吊ったまま休みました。

重湯や水は妹がスプーンですくって飲ませてくれ、顔や身体の血や汗は洗面器の水を取り換えて小まめに拭いてくれました。でも、私にとっては地獄のような日々でした。

当然、薬は無く、傷口には赤チンを塗るだけです。さらに、両肘の傷口が塞がり、かさぶたになると、腕が固まって曲がらなくなってしまいます。そうならないために、病院の先生が私の肘を強引に曲げる。再びかさぶたが破れて皮膚が裂け、血が流れ出すのです。曲げた肘は胸にくくられ、翌日はまた強引に伸ばし、その繰り返しが続きました。一週間以上経ってやっと、自力で肘の曲げ伸ばしができるようになりました。

八月十五日、終戦を迎えた。
何の治療法もなく、ただ傷口に赤チンを塗るだけの手当てで、岩永さんはだんだんと体力が衰えてきた。毎日、髪の毛が両手いっぱいに抜け、歯

茎から血が出た。腕や腿に赤い斑点が出始めた。この斑点が出ると助からないと言われていた。

岩永さんはとうとう、水も飲めなくなるほど弱った。新興善国民学校が救護所になっており、大学病院の医師が治療に当たっているというので、岩永さんはそちらに移ることになった。医師からも、「諦めてください」と言われていたそうだ。といっても、誰もが助からないと思っていた。

私も、「もうここには戻られんとばいねえ」と思い、「うちが死んだらみんなで分けんね」と、小さい頃から大切にしていた人形や、ためていたきれいな千代紙を妹と弟にすべて渡しました。

救護所へ出発する日は戸板に乗せられて、私は見納めになるだろう家の周りの様子を、横になったまま眺めていました。

私は長女で、当時、下に妹が三人、弟が二人いました。みんな、泣きな

がら見送ってくれました。近所の人たちも、道端に並んで送ってくれたように記憶しています。

　救護所といっても国民学校の校舎です。ベッドなどはなく、床にむしろを敷き、そこに家で用意してくれた布団を敷いて横になるだけでした。

　私は二階の教室に入れられ、窓側だったので何げなく外を見ると、トラックが停まっていて、戸板に乗せられた遺体を運んでいるところでした。トラックの荷台には半裸の遺体が積み重なっていました。

　運んできたばかりの遺体を荷台に移すとき、胴体から骸骨化した頭部だけがゴロリと落ちるところを、私は目撃してしまいました。私もああなるんだろうかと恐怖心がつのりました。

　私が救護所に着いて一時間もしないうちに、アメリカの病院船が医薬品を積んで入港したという知らせがあり、着いたばかりの私たちから治療を

受けることになりました。

 私の場合は、薬を塗るという治療ではなく輸血でした。毎日、輸血を受けると、それが効いて、ぐんぐん快方に向かいました。四十五日目には、ついに自宅に戻れるようになったのです。歩いて帰ってきた私を、両親をはじめ、家族みんなが驚いて迎えてくれました。

 防空壕に避難していたときに、頭の地肌が見えるほど毛が抜け、丸坊主になりましたが、深堀の自宅に戻ってからも髪の毛は容赦なく抜けました。髪が生えてきても産毛のようで頭を見ると悲しくなり、外出はできませんでした。

 私は、本当は小学校の先生になりたかったのです。近所の同級生と、「一緒に先生になろうね」などと話し合っていたので、彼女が先生になったと聞いたときは、喜んであげなければならないのに、正直、悲しい気持ちになりました。

岩永さんは実家で一年ほど静養した。その後、親類の病院で二年ほど看護の手伝いをした後、郵便局に勤めた。郵便局で二年働いた頃（昭和二十六年）、母の知人の紹介で、夫とお見合いをして結婚。岩永さんは二十三歳だった。

　私の周囲だけだったのかもしれませんが、被爆の放射能の影響について、それほど問題になっていませんでした。だから、私は主人にも被爆のことを話さなかったし、主人にも聞いたことがなかったのです。後で知ったのですが、夫も被爆者でした。三菱兵器工場の分工場が堂崎（どうざき）にあり、主人は魚雷の試験場で働いていたそうです。原爆投下のその日から堂崎の職場から市内に入り、死体の後始末をしていたので、入市（にゅうし）被爆です。主人は、

「とても臭うて、酒でも飲まんと(死体の)後始末なんてやっとられんやった」

と、話してくれたことがありました。なんでも、工場内には軍隊の隠匿物資の高級ウイスキーやブランデーが大量に置いてあったそうです。

放射能の影響か、主人はいつも「からだの痒いか(体が痒い)」と言っており、二〇〇二年に亡くなりました。

消防団として爆心地に何度も入って救助活動していた父は胆嚢がんで亡くなり、下の弟は大腸がん、胃がんと入退院を繰り返しています。私に付き切りで看病してくれた末の妹は不整脈、心臓肥大、狭心症で苦しんでいます。

私は、二〇〇六年に体調を崩したのを機に原爆症の認定を受けました。このときは、一週間くらい、原因不明の高熱が続きました。この夏(二〇

一四年)も心不全で病院へ。検査の結果、心臓弁膜症との診断。高齢のため、手術は検討中。

二〇一一年には不整脈で入院。退院直前に大腸がんが発見され、半年後には皮膚がんの手術をしました。放射能を受けた身体は、いつも死と隣り合わせです。「もう助からない」と言われながらの七十年でしたが、いまも放射能との戦いは続いているのです。

父母と弟、三人の妹は広島で被爆、三日後に祖母と私は長崎で被爆

梅林二也 さん

うめばやし・つぎや　一九三四年（昭和九年）十二月生まれ。十歳のとき、爆心地から四・五キロ離れた日ノ出町の川で遊んでいて被爆。両親と弟妹は広島で被爆した。長崎大学教育学部を卒業後、土井之首小学校の教員となり七年間、勤めた。その後、団体職員となり、現在も元気で働いている。八十歳。長崎市椎の木町在住。

死体の臭いがいたるところに漂っていた

昭和十九年（一九四四）、広島市観音国民学校四年生だった梅林二也さんは、広島市の爆心地から数キロの観音新町に住んでいた。三菱造船長崎造船所に勤めていた父が、広島に転勤になり家族で引っ越してきたのだ。

梅林さんは三男で、当時十歳。八歳と七歳の妹、四歳の弟、生後数カ月の妹がいた。

空襲が激しくなると、学童の集団疎開が始まった。田舎に親戚がある者は「縁故疎開」、縁故のない者は他の生徒たちと一緒に「集団疎開」となった。

私は両親と離れて、広島県比婆郡西城にある田舎のお寺に疎開しました。生まれて初めての集団疎開は寂しく、そのうえ食料不足でいつもお腹を空

食事は、山で採ってきたフキやワラビ、ゼンマイなどの山菜がどっさり入った雑炊。それでもお腹が空くので、よく山に生えているイタドリの皮を剝(む)いて、酸っぱい茎をかじっていました。

また、天気の良い日には、シャツの縫い目に一列に並んでモソモソ動いているシラミを爪の先で潰(つぶ)したりしたことが思い出されます。

両親に出す手紙は引率の先生の検閲があり、両親が心配するから「寂しい」とか、不満を書いてはいけないと言われていました。

楽しみだったのは、時々、両親から慰問品が送られてくることでした。たいてい乾パンで、私は慰問品がまだ届いていない子に分けてやったりしました。

当時、長崎に祖母がいて、両親に「寂しいから、誰か一人孫をよこすよ

うに」と手紙を書いてきた。そこで、集団疎開していた梅林さんが行くことになった。二カ月の集団疎開から縁故疎開に変わり、長崎で暮らすことになったのだ。

昭和二十年（一九四五）八月九日、あの日は朝からよく晴れていて、私は町内の人たちが掘った防空壕近くの川で遊んでいました。椎の木川の上流で、急に川幅が広がっているので「ひょうたん川」と呼ばれていた川で、近所の子ども二人と川エビを捕っていたのです。

朝方、空襲警報が鳴ったので外に出られず我慢していましたが、警報が解除になり、誘い合って川に向かいました。ひょうたん川は膝までぐらいしか水がない浅い川で、岸の下に網を入れガサガサかき回すと面白いほど川エビが入りました。

夢中で遊んでいると突然、稲妻のような閃光（せんこう）がピカッと光りました。あ

わてて防空壕に駆け込むと、その直後に、「ドカーン」という、凄い音がしたのです。

防空壕の天井の土砂が、体が埋まるほど落ちてきました。防空壕といっても、勤労奉仕で町内の人たちが掘った洞穴なので、いまにも崩れそうでした。

恐怖心と土砂で動けず、そのまましばらくじっとしていると、一緒に遊んでいた子の母親たちが探しに来て、私たちを土砂から掘り出してくれました。

そのとき、私は初めて外を見ました。防空壕に埋まってから一時間ぐらい経っていたでしょうか、あれだけ明るかった夏の空が、夜と間違えるほど真っ暗なのです。

そして、あちこちから火が出て燃え広がっていきました。

祖母が梅林さんを防空壕に探しに来てくれて、一緒に家に帰ったが、途中の家々は屋根瓦が崩れ落ち、ガラスが砕けて飛び散り、吹き飛ばされた家具が路上に散乱していた。

長崎は山が多いのですが、私たちが住んでいた日ノ出町も、「ドンの山」の陰になっていたので家屋の倒壊は免れました。「ドンの山」というのは、お昼になると山の上にある大砲が「ドン」とお昼を知らせるところからこの名が付いた山です。余談ですが、数キロ離れて対面している鍋冠山（なべかんむり）に鉄塔があって、ドンが鳴ると、この鉄塔の丸い鉄球がスーッと下に落ちる仕掛けになっていました。

この「ドンの山」がなかったら、ひょうたん川にいた私たちは、爆風でひとたまりもなかったと思います。

同じ爆弾が広島にも落とされていたことを二、三日後に知り、広島の両親や弟妹たちが無事かどうか心配になりました。

「広島は全滅らしい」という噂が入ると不安と焦りでじっとしていられず、私と祖母は、長崎駅まで行くことにしました。数年前まで長崎に住んでいたのですから、きっと祖母を頼って訪ねてくると思ったのです。

日ノ出町は、ドンの山のおかげで家屋の倒壊が免れたので、近所の家々にも親類がたくさん頼ってきていました。

私たちは市電の線路跡をたどって長崎駅に向かいました。日ノ出町から石橋の電停を過ぎ、出島、大波止に向かうに従って家屋の被害は激しく、建物が吹き飛ばされて原形をとどめていません。一瞬、どこを歩いているのかさえ、分からなくなるほどでした。あちこち、瓦礫で塞がれていて、どこが道路かも判然としません。

荷車が横倒しになり、それを引いていた馬が焼け死んでいました。死体はいたるところに転がっていたのです。

長崎駅とおぼしき場所に来て愕然としました。駅舎は焼けて無くなり、車両も見当たらないのです。駅周辺はほとんど焼け落ち、建物の鉄骨がアメのように曲がって立っているだけでした。

線路の復旧の見込みは立たず、二つ先の道の尾駅で列車は停まったままになっているということでした。ともかく、その日は帰りました。

翌日も、ただ待っていても気がもめるだけなので駅跡に行ってみました。電車は焼け、煤けた状態で停まっています。

血に染まったシャツのまま、放心した姿で歩く人。子どもをおぶって家族の安否を尋ねる人、田舎から親類縁者の家を訪ねてきたのか、倒壊した建物の前で呆然と立ち尽くす人など、町は殺伐とした雰囲気でした。

「救護」の腕章を付けた人が死体を運び、消防団の人が廃材で死体を焼い

ていました。その周りを、散々泣き尽くして、いまさら泣く涙も出ないといった様子で、呆然と肉親の遺体が焼かれる炎を眺めている人たちがいました。

八月十三日、祖母が体調を崩したため駅に迎えに行くのを見合わせた。翌十四日の午後に両親が、弟と三人の妹を連れて、着の身着のままの姿で広島から帰って来た。

八月十一日に広島の宮島を出発したが、広島も被爆しているので列車はスムーズに動かず、四日間かけて長崎・道の尾駅にたどり着いたという。そこからは焼け野原になった長崎の街を、怪我をした弟を父が背負いながら帰って来たのだった。

私は嬉しいというより、驚きの方が大きかったのです。目の前に両親、

妹たちが立っていたのですから。祖母はとても喜んで、とっておいた配給米を炊き、じゃが芋を煮てくれました。いまでも、肉じゃがを食べると、あの日のことが思い出されます。

普段は祖母と二人だけのひっそりとした食卓でしたが、このときは賑やかな雰囲気で、父も母も祖母も互いの無事を喜び合い、大声で話していました。

広島では当初、全員が家の下敷きになったそうですが、幸い父が出勤前で家にいたので、崩れた家の中から一人ひとりを助け出したといいます。妹たちは皆、かすり傷で済みましたが、弟だけは背中に家の梁が落ちてきて大怪我をしました。

父母と弟妹は広島で、祖母と私は長崎で、それぞれ被爆したのです。

しかし、被害が少なく、ともかく無事だったことを、みんなで喜びました。

その後、梅林さんと三人の妹は父の郷里の南島原・布津町に疎開することになり、復旧した列車で向かった。
母は怪我をした弟と長崎の祖母の家に残った。父は息子たちを実家に預けた後、また広島の造船所に戻ることになっていた。

原爆投下から二週間近く経っているのに、車窓からは、田畑で農作業をしていた人たちの焼死体が放置されたままになっているのが見えました。黒焦げの死体の口の辺りから、白い泡みたいなものが垂れ下がっているのが気になりましたが、「あれはウジ虫ではないだろうか」と、後になって気がつきました。
列車内も異常でした。夏の暑い盛りなので手足の火傷の傷口が腐り、そこにハエが飛んできます。ハエは追い払っても、追い払っても飛んでくる

のです。見ると、傷口には白いウジ虫が蠢いていて、母親らしき人が箸でつまんで取っていました。「傷口のウジ虫が動くとすごく痛い」と、その人は言っていました。

しきりに洗面器に血を吐いている人、頭の毛が焼けてしまって男か女か分からない人たち。その臭気で、私は気持ちが悪くなりました。それらに混じって死体の臭い。死体の臭いは一種独特で、何とも言えない嫌な臭いなのです。あの年は、そんな死体の臭いがいたるところに漂っていました。

半年ほどして、梅林さんと妹たちは南島原から長崎に戻った。弟は背中の傷口が化膿して脊椎カリエスに罹っていた。母は、弟の看病のため病院に泊まり込みとなり、梅林さんは母に弁当を届けるために病院に通った。

弟の左腕の火傷は、化膿してなかなか治りませんでした。また、弟は脊椎カリエスで背骨が曲がってしまいましたが、そのまま病状はとまり、いまも元気です。

広島で被爆した三人の妹たちもかわいそうです。どこがどうということはないのですが、いつも体調がすぐれず、年齢とともに寝込む日も多くなったようです。

私はその後、長崎大学教育学部を卒業し、昭和三十二年（一九五七）四月から長崎市内の土井之首小学校の教員となり七年間、奉職しました。その後、団体職員となり、退職後も日常生活には支障なく活動しています。

被爆の症状は、南島原に疎開している頃はずっとありました。だるくて起きていられず、すぐに横になることが多かったのです。しかも、歯茎から血が出て、いつも口の中が気持ち悪いのです。この症状は、長崎に戻ってからもしばらく続きました。また、早い時期から高血圧で、薬を手放せ

ませんでした。

「原爆が伝染る」とひどい差別を受ける

中尾安子 さん

なかお・やすこ　一九三九年（昭和十四年）七月生まれ。爆心地より一・八キロの西坂国民学校近くで、近所の子どもたちと遊んでいるときに被爆。祖母の家や、父の実家などで暮らした後、父が長崎市内に建てたバラックに住む。西坂国民学校に入学。被爆者の夫と結婚。六十八歳まで元気に働いた。七十五歳。長崎市深堀町在住。

五人姉妹の三女として生まれた中尾安子さんは、両親と十二歳と十歳の姉、四歳と三歳の妹の七人で、西坂国民学校の近くで暮らしていた。姉妹はいつも一緒で仲が良く、賑やかだった。

西坂国民学校の隣に建っていた家は畑に囲まれていて、家の上は山になっていた。山の頂上付近に防空壕があったが、そこへ行くには学校の脇から急な石の階段を登って行かなければならなかった。その頃の父は兵器工場に勤めていて、ほとんど帰ってこない生活が続いていた。

極度の恐怖で声も出せなかった

当時、警戒警報が出ると、すぐに空襲警報に変わりました。空襲は、たいてい夜中で、編隊を組んでB29がやって来て、真っ赤に焼けた焼夷弾をバラバラと落とすのです。焼夷弾が落ちると、そこはたちまち燃え上がり

ました。
　最初のうちは空襲警報が出ると、家族全員で防空頭巾を被り、私が位牌を詰めたリュックを背負って、姉たちがそれぞれ一人ずつ妹を連れて避難していましたが、母が身重だったこともあり、山の上の防空壕までなかなかたどり着けませんでした。また小さい子の手を引いてウロウロしていたら、防空壕へ着く前に焼け死んでしまうかもしれないと思い、「どうせ死ぬなら、母子一緒に死のう！」と決め、母を中心に、夜はどんなことがあっても避難しなくなりました。
　あの八月九日、母は早朝から、町内の人たちと山の上の防空壕の修理に出ていました。どの家も、大人は防空壕の修理に駆り出され、家に残された子どもたちは十数人いたと思います。
　朝、空襲警報が出て、姉が私たちを連れて一度、防空壕に避難しましたが、その後、警戒警報に変わったので防空壕を出て家に戻り、その後は近

所の子どもたちと家の前の空き地でままごとをしていました。

午前十一時過ぎ、急に目の前が真っ白になり、すぐに真っ暗になりました。後から思うと、原爆の光があまりにも強烈で、しばらくは周りがまったく見えなかったのだと思います。

ようやく辺りが見えるようになると、景色は一変していました。家は潰れ、屋根瓦が剥がれ、家の障子戸や窓枠、台所にあった梅干しの壺まで外に散乱していました。

気づくと、私も爆風に吹き飛ばされていました。次姉は飛ばされた何かが頭に当たったらしく、血を流していました。あまりの恐ろしさからか、次姉は頭から血を流しているにもかかわらず、「痛い」とも言いませんでした。一緒に遊んでいた子どもたちも誰一人泣いている子はいませんでした。極度の恐怖に誰も声が出ず、泣くという感情さえも起こってこなかったのだと思います。

周りの変わり果てた景色を目の当たりにした姉や年長の子たちが、みんなを連れて母たちが修理に行っている山の防空壕を目指しました。飛び散った瓦礫や倒れた建物で道が塞がれ、まともに歩けませんでした。

途中、貯水池の中で男の人が、泣きながら竹の棒で池をかき回していました。

「なんばしよっと？」と聞くと、

「一緒に畑で仕事ばしよった子どもんおらんごとなった」と言うのです。その子は貯水池の底に叩き付けられて亡くなっていたことを、私は後になって知りました。

飛び散った瓦礫などを避けながら、普段なら十数分で行けるところを、一時間近くかかって防空壕にたどり着きました。

たどり着いた防空壕に、母はいませんでした。母は大きなお腹をかかえながらも、防空壕の天井が崩れないように支える丸太を、学校脇の空き地

64

から近所の人たちと担ぎ、石段を登っている最中だったのです。爆風で一気に排水溝まで飛ばされたということでしたが、流産もせず、怪我もありませんでした。妹たちは、母の顔を見るなり初めて泣き出したのです。

長崎の地形の関係上、爆心地周辺の状況は、私たちには見えませんでした。何があったのかも分かりませんでした。

九日の夕方、長崎駅付近から黒い煙が立ちのぼり、炎が斜面を凄い勢いで登り、残った家も次々と燃えだし、夜になると火の海となりました。

防空壕の中の人たちは口々に、「家ん燃えよる！ うちんがた燃えよる！」と、呻くように呟いていました。その火が西坂国民学校に燃え移ったときには、防空壕の中に大きなため息が響きました。

そして最後に、山の上のわが家も炎に包まれたのです。私たちは自分の家が燃えていくのを、防空壕の前の畑から眺めていました。その火は、夜

65　中尾安子

中でも赤々と燃え、まるで昼間のような明るさでした。その様子をただ呆然と見ているだけでした。

家が燃えてしまったので、中尾さんたちはしばらく防空壕で生活した。防空壕の中は人でいっぱいで、体を伸ばす隙間さえない。姉妹は母のお腹を押さないように気をつけながら、母にもたれかかった。妹たちは母の膝枕で寝ていた。

夕方になって涼しくなると、何人かの人たちは防空壕から出て、B29がいつ来るともしれない恐怖におびえながらも畑や木の根元で横になり、手足を伸ばした。

夏の盛りで畑にはナスやトマト、さつま芋がなっていた。煮炊きの道具もないので、ナスもさつま芋も生のままかじった。「放射能まみれの作物を、そのまま食べていたと思うとゾーッとする」と、中尾さんは振り返

兵器工場で働いていた父とは二日間会えず、家族はてっきり死んだと思って悲しんでいた。ところが思いがけず、足を怪我した父が命からがら戻ってきたのだ。

父は、戻ってくる途中で見た光景を話した。

「水くれ、水くれ！」と水を欲しがってさまよう人たちがそのまま流されていた、と。赤ん坊にお乳を含ませたまま亡くなった母親。焼け爛（ただ）れてズル剝（む）けの顔は男か女かも分からない、それでも呻くように「熱い、熱いよ！」と叫ぶ人々。それはまさに生き地獄のようだった、と話した。

中尾さんの家の、さらに上の方に祖母の家があった。そこは幸い、崖と道路に阻まれていたため火が届かなかった。祖母の家が焼けずに残ったので、父が戻ってきてからは市内の親類四家族二十人が身を寄せ、しばらく

中尾安子

そこで雑魚寝をして暮らした。

子孫には被爆の苦しみを味わわせてはならない

八月十五日、玉音放送で終戦ということを知りましたが、そのときの私は、終戦の意味すら理解できませんでした。しかし大人たちはB29がもう来ないという安心感があったようです。

終戦の翌日だったと思いますが、被爆のときは悲鳴も泣き声も上げなかった私が、雨も降らないのに雷だけがゴロゴロと鳴ったときに、飛び上がるほど怖くて悲鳴を上げました。一緒にいた大人たちも、また敵機が来たと思い、父などはいちばん下の妹を横抱きにして飛び出していったほどでした。

私たち一家は、八月末に父の実家に疎開するため、大波止の港から船に

乗りました。いまなら、車で一時間余りで着くところですが、その頃は道路整備がされてなく、船で行きました。途中までしか船が行かないので、船を乗り継いで行きました。船はだんだんと小さくなり、最後には私たち家族だけが手漕ぎボートで上陸しました。

船には怪我をした人が大勢乗っていました。当時、長崎には遠方の島の人たちが学徒動員でたくさん来ていましたが、その人たちが被爆し、島から両親や親類の人たちが連れ戻しに来ていました。ろくに手当てを受けないまま乗せられたのか、傷口は焼け爛れたまま、ハエがブンブンと群がっています。

そのなかには、すでに死んでいる人が何人もいました。死んでいるわが子を、「せめて故郷で土葬に」と思っているのでしょうか、死体は担架や毛布に包んでありました。かわいそうだという思いもありましたが、それ以上に、凄い臭いに耐えられず、私は一刻も早く船を降りたいと思いまし

中尾安子

た。
　やっとの思いで父の実家に着いたものの、「原爆を受けた」というだけで、私たちはひどい扱いを受けました。
　父の実家は長崎市内から遠く離れた田舎なので、被爆した人はおらず、私たちの苦しみは理解されませんでした。私たち家族は、「原爆が伝染る」といって毛嫌いされ、父の実家の人たちも村人の手前、母屋どころか離れにも上げてくれません。
　私たちには農具や肥料が入れてある納屋が与えられ、小屋の周りの畑を貸してもらって、自分たちで野菜を植えて食べるという生活をしました。父は仕事があるのですぐに長崎に戻って行き、女だけの家族になると差別はますますひどくなりました。
　お正月の終わりに、村では松飾りなどの正月飾りを焼く行事、どんど焼きが行われました。

その賑やかな雰囲気を感じると、私や妹は行ってみたくてたまらなくなるのですが、父の実家からは、「村の人たちがいる間は小屋から出ないように」と言われていました。

母に行きたいとせがむと、「(実家に)世話になっとるけん、しょうがなか」と、寂しそうに言うばかりです。

長姉がときどき偵察に行って、村の人たちがいなくなるのを見届けると、私たちを連れてどんど焼きの場所に連れて行ってくれました。火はすでに消え、焼け跡になっていました。

小屋のすぐ裏はきれいな砂浜で、暗くなって浜に人がいなくなった頃、姉が貝掘りに連れ出してくれました。さんざん採られた後で、貝はほとんどありませんでしたが、小さな貝を採ったり、砂遊びをしたり、妹たちは嬉しそうでした。私も、つかの間の楽しみを味わいました。きれいな貝殻を拾って帰り、家の中で遊んだりもしました。

そんななか、この年の十月に弟が生まれました。

被爆したことを、伝染病に罹っているかのように思われていたので、母は産婆や助産婦の手を借りずに、この小屋で一人で弟を産みました。

十二歳の長姉と十歳の次姉が母に言われる通り、お湯を沸かしたり布切れを集めたりして母の出産を手伝いました。

弟は、初めての男の子ということで「初男」と名づけられました。

私たち五人の姉は、暇さえあれば初男を取り囲み、母に怒られるほど、代わる代わる触ったり撫でたりしてあやしました。

翌年に、父がバラックを建てたので、家族は長崎に戻った。被爆から八カ月後の四月の長崎は、まだ焼け野原だった。

昭和二十一年（一九四六）、私は西坂国民学校に入学しました。学校といっても、急ごしらえの木造で、教室の数も少なく足らなかったため、一年と二年は午前と午後に分かれて登校したり、外の石段に座って授業を受けました。

　そんな物の無いなかを父はどう工面したのか、初男のために紙でできた鯉のぼりを探してきて、家の前に立てた。風になびく色鮮やかな鯉のぼりは、女の子である姉妹にとっても誇らしかったという。またお正月には両親が五人姉妹全員に洋服を新調し、毬や羽子板を買ってくれた。喧嘩しないように、大きさも絵柄もだいたい同じものだったが、「私の方はこう、お姉ちゃんの方はどう？」と、姉妹で比べ合った。

中尾安子

弟の初男は一歳の伝い歩きする年齢になっても、二、三歩歩くとすぐにドンと尻餅をついていました。変だと思っていると、お腹の両脇に大きなおできができて赤く腫れあがり、やがて破けて膿が出てきました。痛いのでギャーギャー泣いていました。小さな体に大きなおできが、かわいそうでした。

病院で切ってもらい、膿を出した後にガーゼを詰めるのですが、傷口がポッカリと穴になっていて、とても痛そうでした。

医師には、「十歳までは生きられないだろう」と言われました。ところが、しばらくしておできは完治したのです。

けれど、その影響で背骨が曲がったままになりました。また心筋梗塞や脳梗塞などを次々と発症したのです。胎内被爆の影響でしょうか。

私は学校を卒業するとさまざまな仕事をしましたが、最後は中華菓子の

製造で六十八歳まで働きました。

主人も被爆者ですが、結婚するときも被爆のことは気にしませんでした。一時、「被爆者には奇形児が生まれる」という噂もありましたが、姉の子たちも元気に生まれたので、私も妊娠したときに気にもしませんでした。私の子ども、孫たちもおかげさまで元気です。

父、長姉、次姉は心臓病で、母は肝臓がんと膵臓がんで、一番下の妹は子宮がんと大腸がんで亡くなりました。

いろんな病気をし、十歳までは生きられないだろうと言われた弟は、いまも元気にやっています。私とすぐ下の妹は何の病気もなく今日まで元気です。

子や孫や、後に続く世代には、私たちが経験した苦しみを決して味わわせてはならない、といつも思っています。

中尾安子

祈りを込めて「原爆死没者名簿」を筆耕

谷川正潤 さん

たにがわ・まさひろ　一九三七年(昭和十二年)十二月生まれ。爆心地から四キロの西小島の自宅近くで七歳のときに被爆。定時制高校で学びながら長崎市役所に勤務。卒業後も同じ職場で働き、表彰状などを書き上げる仕事に携わることもあった。退職後は学校から卒業証書を書く仕事などを依頼される。現在は、「長崎原爆の日」に奉安される「原爆死没者名簿」の筆耕を行う(現在、妻の看病のため一時休止中)。七十七歳。長崎市葉山在住。

防空壕の近くで妹たちとトンボ捕りをしていて被爆

谷川正潤さんは九人きょうだい（兄五人、姉一人、妹二人）の下から三番目。母は再婚で、前夫との間に四人、長崎税関に勤める谷川さんの父との間に五人の子どもがいた。

一家が住む西小島は、日本で最初の西洋医学校である医学伝習所が設けられた、オランダ医学の発祥の地。近くには丸山遊郭の街並みもあり、歴史ある町だ。

谷川さんの長兄は兵隊に行っており、次兄は戦死、四男は昭和十六年（一九四一）に病死していた。三番目の兄は長崎で消防隊員として勤めており、佐古国民学校の二年生（七歳）だった谷川さんは、すぐ上の兄（五男・小学校六年生）と、五歳と二歳の妹の四人で、いつも仲良く遊んでいた。

あの日、母は勤労奉仕で早朝から町内の「防空壕掘り」に出かけ、私たち兄妹四人は空襲警報が鳴ったために家にいました。やがて、警報は解除となり、「母さんのおるところへ行ってみようや」ということになって、みんなで母のいるところへ向かいました。

「防空壕掘り作業」は、家から二百メートルほどのところで、当時、男はみんな兵隊に行っているので婦人だけで作業をしていました。雁爪（がんづめ）(先が熊手のような形になった農器具)で土を掘り、その土を竹のかごに詰めて外に運び出すという作業です。

昼休みにはまだ時間があったので、私は防空壕の近くの空き地で二人の妹たちにトンボを捕ってやっていました。

そのとき、ピカッという稲妻のような閃光（せんこう）が走ったのです。私たちはびっくりして、母たちのいる防空壕に逃げ込みました。音は聞こえませんでした。

「爆弾ばい！」
誰かが叫びました。
幸い、私たちはどこにも怪我はありませんでしたが、次々と怪我をした人たちが防空壕に避難してきます。みんな口々に、「もう、長崎の町は全滅ばい！」と言っていました。
外に出てみると県庁が燃えており、駅前の辺りに黒い雲が覆い被さっていました。
「いま出て行くと危なかけん、しばらくここにおった方がいい」
と言われ、夕方まで母と兄妹で防空壕にいましたが、自宅が心配で戻った人たちもいたようです。
夕方になると、父が防空壕に来ました。頭に白いカーテン生地をターバンのように巻いていて、それが血で真っ赤に染まっているのです。父は職場の長崎税関で、爆風によるガラスの破片で怪我をしたのでした。

谷川正潤

夜になり、谷川さんは両親、兄妹の六人で家に戻った。家は傾いたり、屋根が飛ばされたりということもなく、無事だった。

消防署（爆心地から二キロ）に勤務していた三番目の兄は、署内で爆風に飛ばされたがどこにも怪我はなく、すぐに浦上方面に救助活動に出かけた。夜になって上司から「家族の安否確認」の許可が出たため自宅に帰ってきたが、家族の無事を確認すると安心して再び救助活動に戻って行った。

兄たちは、次々と亡くなっていく人たちの死体処理を行っていたそうです。

私の記憶でも、自宅近くの館内市場跡（現・十善会病院付近）が死体焼却場になっており、運び込まれて順番を待っている死体が並べられていました。

最初は、裸同然の死体が多かったのですが、順番を待つ間に、死体には浴衣や上着が掛けられました。裸のままでは不憫と思い、衣類を掛けてあげる人たちがいたのでしょう。

家の柱や梁を運んできて井桁に組み、その上に死体を乗せ、昼夜を問わず焼き続けていました。一晩中、死体を焼く炎の光と臭いは、いまでも忘れることができません。

一度に何人もの死体を焼き、その周囲には身内の人がズラリと並んで焼けるのを待っているのです。どれが誰の骨やら分からないなか、各自が持ってきた入れ物に骨を入れて帰って行きました。

それから二、三日後、「進駐軍が上陸してくる。女、子どもは皆殺しにされる」という噂が流れました。近所の人たちは、それぞれ親類を頼って逃げ出したのです。私たちも母の遠い親戚がいる西有家町（現・南島原市）に疎開することにしました。

谷川正濶

長崎駅が焼けて汽車が出ないので、十四日の夕方、家族六人で出発。夜通し歩いて、十五日の明け方に汽車の通っている諫早に、やっと到着しました。

近くのお寺で休ませてもらいましたが、避難してきた人で溢れかえっていました。そのときにいただいた、おにぎりのおいしかったことは忘れられません。

そのお寺で、私は玉音放送を聞きました。

諫早からは汽車で西有家まで行きました。本家というだけあって大きな農家で、私は妹たちと広い庭で遊んでいました。すでにあちこちから親類が避難してきており、「あんたたちのいる場所はなかばい」と言われ、その夜、一晩泊まっただけで、私たちはまた長崎の自宅に再び戻ることになりました。帰りの汽車の中で、父が不機嫌だったことを覚えています。

投下直後の町は、瓦礫と焼け跡のくすぶった煙で廃墟のようでした。

周りは、男女の区別がつかないほど焦げた死体、片腕がちぎれて皮膚一枚で繋がっている人、死んだ赤ん坊を抱きしめ呆然と歩く母親、飛び出した内臓を片手で押さえて苦しんでいる人などでいっぱいとのことでした。倒れている人たちが口々に、「水くれ〜、水くれ〜」と呻いています。

当初は、西小島の被害が少ないのは爆心地から四キロも離れているせいかと思っていましたが、その辺りは手前が小高い丘のようになっていて、丘に隠れるように家が建っていたので家屋の被害が少なかったのです。

ところが同じように四キロ離れていても、平坦な場所では爆風の直撃で建物倒壊の被害が大きかったのでした。

消防隊員として救助活動に当たった兄から後で聞いた話では、「浦上方面に救助に向かったが電車の架線は垂れ下がり、民家、学校、工場などの建物が燃えたり倒れたりしていた。水道管が破裂していて救助活動ができ

ないありさまだった」ということでした。その兄（三男）は肺がんで、私たちと一緒にいたすぐ上の兄（五男）は心臓病で亡くなりました。父母も妹たちも、被爆による後遺症が無かったのは不思議なことです。

兄たちが亡くなったこともあり、心配した父に言われて谷川さんは二十代半ばで被爆者手帳を申請した。申請には保証人（証明者）が二人必要だった。近所の人はほとんど引っ越してしまい、しかも二十年近く経っているので、子どもの頃の谷川さんを知っている人は、すでにいなくなっており、探すのに苦労した。

谷川さんは定時制高校に入り、昼間は市役所に勤務。高校卒業後もそのまま市役所に勤め続けた。文字を書くのが好きだった谷川さんは、正式に毛筆や硬筆を習ったことはなかったものの、市役所勤務時代から、「字がきれいだから」と表彰状などを書く仕事をよく頼まれた。退職後は、自治

会の感謝状や学校の卒業証書などを頼まれるようになった。

西海（さいかい）出身の妻と結婚。妻は被爆していないが、被爆者の谷川さんとの結婚を反対した妻の親類はいない。

私は二〇〇六年から、長崎市の依頼を受けて八月九日の「長崎原爆の日」に奉安される「原爆死没者名簿」の筆耕を行っています。書き始めの頃、心臓の手術のため入院したすぐ上の兄（五男）を見舞い、筆耕のことを報告すると、「大事なことやけん、頑張って書けよ」と励まされました。

その後、兄は急遽（きゅうきょ）手術することになり、その二週間後に亡くなったのです。よもや、筆耕の最初の年に兄の名前を書くことになろうとは、夢にも思いませんでした。

この依頼を受けてから今日まで、筆耕の数日前には必ず原爆資料館を訪

れるようにしています。展示物を見て死没者のことを思いつつ、「平和を願い、亡くなった方々のご冥福を祈り、筆を握らせてもらいます」と、深く祈っています。

私が書いた名前、享年、死没年月日は永遠に残ります。自然と、「丁寧に書かなければ」と、気持ちが引き締まります。

そして、毎年、八月九日の式典で無事に奉安されたときは、心からほっとするのです。

「被爆語り継ぎの本つくる」と娘に言われ、長い沈黙を破る

高比良信治 さん

たかひら・のぶはる　一九二八年（昭和三年）十二月生まれ。十六歳のとき爆心地から三キロの長崎港近くの三菱電機の工場で被爆。被爆後は体調が思わしくなく、心に不安をかかえて生きてきた。勤労奉仕をした三菱電機で定年まで勤め上げる。次女から「被爆の語り継ぎの文集を作る」と言われ、初めて被爆体験を語った。八十六歳。長崎市界町在住。

怪我そのものより「心の不安」が被爆者の深い苦しみ

仁田国民学校高等科二年生で、卒業を四カ月後に控えていた高比良信治さんは、勤労奉仕のため、長崎港近くにある三菱電機の工場で船舶用のモーターの固定部分と回転部分をつなぐ作業に携わっていた。

朝からよく晴れた日で、高比良さんは作業中に一度、B29爆撃機の爆音を聞き工場の窓から空を見上げたが、何も見えなかったという。

そのついでに、「何時やろか？」と工場の入り口の上部にある時計を見た瞬間、ピカッと、横に長く真っ白な光が広がったのです。光の方向に顔を向けたとたん、ドカーンという、もの凄い音を聞きました。

とっさに両手の親指で耳を、人差し指と中指で目を押さえ地面に伏せました。日頃から、耳の鼓膜と目を守る防災訓練として、作業中に抜き打ち

89　高比良信治

で、担当の軍属が「伏せ！」と言い、私たちにそのような姿勢を取らせていたので、素早い行動が取れたのです。

同時に、天井の高い工場の窓ガラスが音をたてて落ちてきました。頭には戦闘帽を被り、作業着を着ていたので、頭や体は何ともありませんでしたが、右耳の後ろに尖ったガラスの破片が突き刺さり、温かい血がダラダラと顔の方に流れてくるのを感じました。あと少しそれて首の頸動脈に刺さっていたらと思うと「ゾーッ」とします。その傷は、いまも残っています。

高比良さんが伏せた顔を上げると、爆風で屋根はすべて吹き飛ばされ、建物は鉄骨だけになって青空が見えていた。工場内のごみや塵が、もうっと上空へ吹き上げられている。

工場の反対側には、女工さんだけの木造の作業場が一棟あり、熊本女

学校の挺身隊が研修に来て、探照灯（サーチライト）の製造に当たっていた。木造だったため、かなりの人が亡くなったそうだ。

　工場内にいた工員たちが、一斉に工場裏手の防空壕へ走っていくのが見えました。防空壕といっても、山の斜面の岩石をくり抜いて造った、大型タービン発電機の試験場として使っていたところです。そこに、工場に勤めていた千二百余人が一気に押しかけてきたのです。
　私のように工場内で作業をしていた者は、窓ガラスが突き刺さったり、吹き飛ばされた物に当たって怪我をしたりで、血を流している人が多かったのですが、外で作業をしていた人たちはもっと悲惨でした。髪の毛はちりちりに焦げ、皮膚は焼け爛れて、衣服はぼろぼろになっていました。
　また、防空壕の中ではほとんどの人が、真夏だというのに「寒気がする」と、ぶるぶる震えていました。

高比良信治

自宅に帰ろうと工場を出たときに見た光景は、信じられないものでした。われ先に逃げる人たちに混じって、焼け爛れて幽霊のような格好でふらふら歩く人や、死んだ赤ん坊を抱きしめたまま、うわ言のように何かを喚き散らしている女性などが、うろうろしていたのです。そして、私は、やっと稲佐橋(いなさばし)まで来ることができました。

昼食前の時間帯で食事の支度をしていた家が多かったためか、あちこちから火が出て、みるみるうちに燃え広がり、浦上方面は火の海になった。最初は木造の民家が燃え、夕方頃になって会社が入っているビル等が燃えだした。

見ると、路面電車が箱ごと吹き飛ばされ、剥(む)き出しのトロッコのような電車の線路はジェットコース床の上に乗客が折り重なって死んでいます。

ターのようにうねって盛り上がられた死体も転がっていました。

稲佐橋から先へ行くのは無理と判断し、市営船で対岸の上小島(かみこしま)にある自宅に帰ろうと思い、私は引き返して大波止(おおはと)桟橋(さんばし)に向かいました。

ところが、市営船の船長が逃げてしまって、船は出ないというのです。

そのとき、上空に敵機が現れ、凄い勢いで機銃を撃ってきました。

不意の機銃掃射に逃げまどい、皆、桟橋の下に隠れたり床に伏せたりしましたが、夏の白い開襟(かいきん)シャツが目立たないわけがないのです。それでも、撃たれた者が出なかったのが、いまも不思議でなりません。

敵機は去りましたが、市営船は出ません。いらいらしていると、いまかしら思うと漫画みたいですが、手漕ぎの伝馬船(てんません)が一艘(そう)、ギーコギーコとやってきたのです。

当時、バス代わりの市営船の他に、手漕ぎの伝馬船を購入して交通手段

に使っている人たちもずいぶんいました。周りの緊張感に比べて間の抜けた光景ですが、長崎市内が心配になった人たちが川を舟で渡って来たところでした。

乗船者が降りると、桟橋にいた私たちがわれ先にと乗り込みましたが、五、六人も乗ればいっぱいです。しかも、船頭がいません。乗り込んだうちの一人が、見よう見まねで櫓を漕ぎ出しました。

船が川の中ほどに来たとき、先ほどの敵機が戻ってきました。さあ、船の中は大騒ぎです。ボートをちょっと大きくしたぐらいの伝馬船の中に、逃げる場所などありません。

「早よせんか！　なんばしよっとか」「右さん回れ（右へ旋回しろ！）」

皆はいろいろ言うのですが、漕いでいるのも素人なのですっかり気が動転しています。あわてて手首をどこかにぶつけたのか、その人の腕時計のバンドが切れて海中へ落ちたのです。すぐに拾おうとして身を乗り出した

拍子に、素人船頭本人まで海に落ちてしまったのです。上空の敵機を目で追いながら私たちが彼を引き上げたとき、今度は、伝馬船の櫓が留め金から外れて、船は流れのままに漂うしかありませんでした。

敵機は空高く上がり、一度エンジンを切って音を消し、一気に降りてくる。船が見える辺りから、失速しないように再びエンジンを掛け、機銃を撃ちながら海面すれすれから再び上昇していく。

当然、私たちは狙われているので、船の中は悲鳴が上がり、大混乱です。誰もが、櫓もなく海上で停まっている船は敵機の的だと思いました。ところが、よく見ると櫓には紐（ひも）がついていて、流されてもたぐり寄せられるようになっていたのです。

いま、話すと滑稽でおかしいのですが、あのときは生死の境でそれどこ

ろではなく、私も船の中で身を縮めて無事に大波止に着くことだけを祈っていました。

海面にピュン、ピュンと、刺さるように撃ち込まれる機銃の音はいまも忘れられません。

不思議なことに、敵機もあわてていたのか新米の兵士だったのか、誰も撃たれず大波止に着き、私はそこから大きく遠回りして上小島の実家に戻りました。

途中、見渡すと大波止の後方（いまの県庁付近）は火の海でした。その火は、三日三晩燃え続け、その後は大雨が数日間、降り続きました。私のいた上小島は、普通の大雨でしたが、黒い雨が降ったところもあったと聞きました。

家に戻ってみると、窓ガラスは全部吹き飛んでいました。ほかには建物

96

が壊れたところはありませんでした。
母は数年前に亡くなり、弟も結核で小さい頃、すでに死亡。ですから、私はずっと印刷所に勤める父と二人きりの生活でした。
私は夕方に着き、夜になって防空壕に避難していた父が家に戻ってきました。
「市内は新型爆弾で全部やられたと聞いとったけん、もう、お前は死んでしもうたて思うとったぞ」と、父はとても喜んでくれました。
三菱電機の工場は破壊されて稼働できず、二年余り閉鎖になっていた。工場が再開されると、高比良さんは再び仕事に戻り、定年まで三菱電機に勤めた。
その間、私は昭和二十八年（一九五三）に結婚しました。妻が住み込みで

働いていたチャンポン専門店を、うちの会社が忘年会や新年会でよく使っていたので、店の女将も私を知っていました。女将と私の叔父が知り合いだったため、ある日、私の見合いの話になりました。

ところが、妻の母から、「貧乏やったちゃ（貧乏でも）健康な人がよかばい」と言われ、当時、顔色の悪かった私は健康診断書を提出させられました。義母は私が被爆者であることを知っていたようです。

妻から聞いた話では、長男が生まれたとき、見舞いに来た義母が妻に気づかれないように赤ん坊の手と足の指を一本一本触って確認していたそうです。やはり、気になっていたのでしょう。

でも、私はあの日は建物内（工場）にいましたし、「放射能のガス」は吸っていないので、影響があるわけないと思っていました。私にとって被爆の影響は、ガラスの破片で切った耳の後ろの傷だけだと思い込んでいたのです。

ところが、工場が再開された年の健康診断で胃潰瘍が見つかりました。この頃から体調が悪くなり、しょっちゅう下痢をしていました。いつも常備薬の頓服「赤玉」という整腸薬を持っていて、よく飲んでいました。それから、甲状腺も弱く、何かあるとすぐに喉が腫れ上がったのです。

「被爆の影響による不安感」については、あまり話したくありません。これだけは、当事者でないと分かっていただけないと思うからです。過酷なものです。ちょっと体調が悪いと胃の辺りがチクチク痛み、「なんか、悪か病気ばせんやろか？（なにか悪い病気では）」と不安になります。被爆者の苦しみというのは火傷や怪我というより、むしろ、そちら（心の不安）の方ではないでしょうか。そんな不安を抱き続けての七十年間でした。

被爆のことは妻に聞かれても、ずっと話しませんでした。思い出したく

なかったからです。
ところが娘が高校生になったとき、「被爆の語り継ぎの本ば作るごとなったけん、話ば聞かせて」と言われ、初めは断っていましたが、とうとう口に出してしまいました。
でも本当は、いまでもできることなら思い出したくはないのです。

被爆を夫に隠し続け、思い悩んだ新婚時代

濱百合代 さん

はま・ゆりよ 一九三五年（昭和十年）十月生まれ。九歳のとき、爆心地から二キロの稲佐町の自宅で被爆。母が被爆で亡くなった後、しばらくはきょうだいだけで飢えをしのいだ。中学卒業後、みかんの缶詰工場に勤めたが、ひどい貧血のため退職。二十二歳で結婚。体調不良で寝込む日が続くが、元気な女児を出産。七十九歳。長崎市琴海太平町在住。

欠けたどんぶりに被爆死した母の遺骨を摘んで入れた

　濱百合代さんは、十五歳の長姉、十三歳の長兄を頭に男三人、女四人の七人きょうだいの上から四番目。当時、九歳だった。父はサイパンに出征しており、母と子どもたちで、稲佐町に暮らしていた。長姉と長兄は三菱造船所に勤労奉仕に通っていた。

　母は体が弱かったので、いつも私を呼んでは身の回りを手伝わせ、「おなごは控えめにしとかんといかんよ」が、口癖でした。

　昭和二十年八月九日、午前十一時二分。その日は警戒警報が解除され、町全体がシーンと静かで、それがかえって不気味な気がしていました。朝、町内から一家族に一合の小豆の配給があり、母がかまどに鍋をかけ、小豆と砂糖の代わりにサッカリンでぜんざいを炊いてくれていました。甘

103　濱百合代

いものが手に入らない時代でしたから、私たちはたとえ一口ずつのぜんざいでも楽しみで、でき上がりを心待ちにしていました。

炊き上がったぜんざいを、「熱いから少し冷ましてから食べさせるね」と母が言った矢先、一瞬、ピカッと光り、「ドカーン」と凄い音がしたのです。

家が壊れ、傾き、母も私たち弟妹も爆風で吹き飛ばされ、母が炊いてくれたぜんざいも一瞬のうちに飛び散ってしまいました。外を見ると、何枚もの衣類が凧のように飛んでいくのが見えました。

私のすぐ下の弟（七歳）は、縁側で寝ていたので全身に大火傷を負いました。

実は、私も最初は涼しい場所を探して一緒に横になっていたのですが、陽が高くなるにつれて暑くなってきたので、起きて部屋に入ったところで

した。顔と手の火傷がひどく、変わり果てた弟の姿に、母は気が狂ったようになっていました。

夕方、姉と兄が勤労奉仕から戻り、私たち母子は夜の明けるのを待って、母の故郷である西彼杵郡外海の叔父（母の弟）の家に行くことにしました。自宅のある稲佐からは八キロもあります。

長姉は全身火傷の弟をおんぶして、途中、背中の弟に何度も「生きとっとね？」「生きとっとね？」と声をかけ、息のあるのを確認しながら歩いていました。

浦上川の大橋のところまで来ると、真っ黒に煤けてアザラシのような人たちの群れが見えました。その人たちは口々に「水、水」と呟きながら、川に入っては流されていくのでした。

弟も喉が渇くのか、しきりに「水! 水!」と、息も絶え絶えになりながら求めるのです。水を飲ませると死んでしまうと聞いていたので、何とかなだめながら歩き、やっと叔父の家に着きました。

外海の叔父の家に着くと、母はすぐに「稲佐の家が気がかりだ」と、壊れた家の後片づけをしに戻って行きました。

そのときに、大量の放射能ガスを吸ったのでしょう。二、三日後、私たち年上のきょうだい四人で稲佐町の自宅に戻ったときには、母の顔には黒い斑点が出ていたのです。その斑点は日ごとに全身に広がっていきました。

母の唇は紫色になり、「きつか(苦しい)! きつか!」と言いながら、水ばかりガブガブ飲んでいましたが、被爆から一週間後の八月十六日に、八人目の子どもを妊娠したまま、母は亡くなりました。

死ぬ直前、「湯飲み茶わん一杯でよかけん、白かご飯ば食べたか」「死に

とうなか、父ちゃんはまだやろうか」と言い続け、ずっと私の手を握り、最後は目玉も飛び出さんばかりに見開いたまま、亡くなったのです。三十三歳でした。色白で小柄な、口数の少ない母でした。

翌日のお昼過ぎ、叔父と私たち年上のきょうだい四人で母の遺体を焼きました。叔父は、遺体に火を付ける瞬間だけは、私たちに見せたくなかったのでしょう。私たちは、遺体から離れるように言われました。火が付けられてしばらくしてから、叔父に呼ばれたのです。燃えている母の遺体を見るのが悲しく、また怖くて早く焼けるように、私たちはどんどん木片をくべました。

三時間か四時間、経ったでしょうか。かなり長い時間がかかったと記憶しています。瓦礫（がれき）の中にあった、欠けたどんぶりに母の骨を一つ一つ摘（つま）んで入れました。数時間前の母の遺体は、たったどんぶり一杯の骨になった

のです。

叔父の家にどんぶりに入れた遺骨を抱いて戻ると、母の死を理解していない幼い弟や妹は、「あーちゃん（お母さん）はどこへ行ったと？」「いつ帰ってくると？」と尋ねます。長姉がぽろぽろ涙をこぼしながら、黙って妹や弟を抱き締めました。

しばらくの間、全身火傷のすぐ下の弟（七歳）とその下の弟（五歳）と妹（三歳）の三人は外海の叔父に預かってもらい、上のきょうだい四人は壊れた稲佐の家で、子どもたちだけで生活した。しかし、電気も水道もない。浮浪児のように、生き残ったそれぞれの仲間と一緒に食べ物を探しに行くといった、荒んだ生活を送った。

それでも、いよいよ困ると、兄や姉が外海の叔父の所へ行ってさつま芋を貰ってきた。家では火を焚くのも大変なので、洗って生のまま食べたと

家の水道は壊れており、兄に言われて焼け跡の水道に水汲みに行こうと外に出ると、家の前に男の人が立っていました。その人が私をじっと見て、
「百合代か？」と言うのです。父でした。玉砕したと聞いていた激戦地のサイパン島から、思いがけず父が帰ってきたのでした。
　しかも、出征前とは別人のような格好でひげを生やして刀を下げ、戦闘帽を被り、まるで大将のようです。嬉しさより、怖さと驚きが先に立ちました。
　父に「母ちゃんは？」と尋ねました。「死んだ」と、私が答えると、何も言わずにうつむいたままじっとしていましたが、しばらくして堰を切ったように泣き出したのです。「アメリカの鼻の高かと（鼻の高い奴）を殺してやる！　家内を返せ！」と叫びながら。

父は生き残った子どもたちのために、傾いた家を建て直した。食べるものがなくなると、外海の実家から芋を貰ってきて子どもたちに食べさせる、という生活が一年余り続いた。

やがて、叔父の紹介で、父はやっと三菱造船所に勤め先が決まったが、妻のいない寂しさを紛らわせるために飲んでいた酒の量が次第に増えて、いつしか外でも飲むようになり、二日酔いで仕事を休む日が多くなっていった。

二、三カ月後、ついに父は工場をクビになってしまい、生活はますます苦しくなった。

被爆の年は夏みかんが豊作で、私たち兄妹はあちこちに生っている夏みかんを勝手にちぎっては、それで飢えをしのいでいました。

そのせいか、近所で物が無くなれば、すぐに私たち兄妹が盗んだように言われたりしました。「こんなとき、母ちゃんがおったら、こげん言われんでもよかとにね」と、皆で泣きました。

被爆したときに大火傷をした弟は全身が水ぶくれになり、顔が腫れ上がって目も開けられず、「何にも見えん」「痛か」と苦しんでいました。とくにひどかった両腕と手の甲にはウジ虫が湧き血膿（ちうみ）が出て、化膿（かのう）したところの肉がえぐられたようになり、ひどい臭いがしました。

「火傷にはじゃが芋の擦った汁が効く」と聞き、外海からじゃが芋を貰ってきては、それを弟に塗ってやるのが私の役目になりました。汁を付けてやると、「しょむか（滲（し）みる）！」「痛か！」と悲鳴を上げて、とてもかわいそうでした。じゃが芋のおかげで一年半ぐらいでずいぶん良くなり、二年遅れて弟は小学校に復学しました。

しかし、頭から顔にかけてのケロイドがひどく、初めて会った人は正直、気持ちが悪くなるほどだったと思います。

そのためか、弟は次第に外に出なくなりました。近所の子どもたちからも、「原子の子」「原子の子」と、いじめられていたようです。

その弟も昭和三十三年（一九五八）、二十歳のときに結婚し、いまでは五人の子どもにも恵まれ、幸せな生活を送っています。けれど、火傷の跡を隠すため、夏でも長袖シャツを着て、ケロイドで引き攣れた手の甲を隠すために手袋を離したことはありません。

私は中学卒業後、稲佐のみかんの缶詰工場に勤めましたが、仕事中、貧血で倒れることが多く、会社に迷惑をかけるのが嫌で退職しました。そんな状態なので、家事をするのも人の二倍も三倍もの時間がかかりました。

弟と同じ昭和三十三年、二十二歳のときに、父の知人の紹介でイワシ漁

の漁師であった夫と結婚。体調の不安もありましたが、「被爆」のことは夫には話さずに結婚しました。

当時、原爆のガスを吸った女性からは奇形児が生まれるという噂が広がっており、被爆していることが分かったら離婚させられるという話だったので、夫にはどんなことがあっても言うまいと決めたのです。

幸せなはずの新婚時代も、目まいと吐き気のため寝込む日が続きました。夫のために食事を作ってあげたいと思い、台所に立つのですが、すぐに血の気が引き、目の前が真っ暗になり、立ちくらみで倒れてしまいます。でも、病院に行くと、「極度の貧血だが、原因は分からない」と言われるだけなのです。

そんな不安な中、病弱ではあっても子どもだけは欲しい、と願っていたところ、私は間もなく妊娠しました。

ある日、主人がどこからか聞いてきたのか、「被爆者には黒い赤ちゃんが生まれるという話だ。おまえは被爆者じゃないだろうな？」と言うのです。
 一瞬、十三年前に被爆したときのことが蘇り、言葉に詰まってしまいました。その場を何と言って取り繕ったのか、覚えていません。
 主人は私を疑って言ったのではなく、親なら誰でも思うように普通の子どもが生まれるかどうか心配だったのでしょう。その気持ちは痛いほど分かりながら、被爆したことを隠したまま過ごさざるを得ませんでした。いまさら言ってみたところで主人を苦しめるだけ。私の胸にしまっておくしかないのです。打ち明けられない分、不安で夜も眠れない日が続きました。
 何も知らない主人は身重の私をいたわってくれ、「寝とけ、寝とけ」と

言って大事にしてくれました。
そんな主人に応えるためにも、健康な子どもが生まれることを必死に願いました。もし、黒い赤ちゃんが生まれたら、そのときはその子と一緒に死のう、と考えていたのです。
その頃はよく、母のお腹の中で、母と共に亡くなった胎児のことばかりを考えていました。
昭和三十四年（一九五九）三月二十三日。病弱な私にしては思ったより安産で、さまざまな不安と葛藤のなかで生まれてきた赤ちゃんは、色白で太った元気な女の子でした。
出産のときに立ち会ってくれた大家の奥さんから、「おなごん子（女の子）の立派な赤ちゃんばい。父ちゃんによう似とるばい」と言われたときは、嬉しくて、嬉しくて、声を上げて泣きました。

115　濱百合代

原爆は女性にむごい。生命を宿す「母」を執拗にいじめ続ける

岩本光子 さん

いわもと・みつこ 一九三七年(昭和十二年)三月生まれ。爆心地から〇・五キロの自宅付近で八歳のときに被爆し、大火傷を負う。両親も妹も亡くなり、一人になる。極度の貧血に苦しむが、二十七歳で結婚。出血多量や新生児の仮死状態など命がけの分娩を乗り越え、一男二女に恵まれた。七十八歳。長崎市女の都在住。

被爆したこと夫には告げず、身ごもったときは不安で眠れなかった

岩本光子さんの父は警察官で、赴任していた朝鮮で数年前に亡くなっていた。母は、三菱製鋼所で働きながら、八歳の岩本さんと六歳の妹を育てていた。

家では、岩本さんの叔母（母の妹）とその三人の娘たちも一緒に暮らした。叔母の夫がフィリピンに出征していたためだ。

私は城山国民学校三年生でした。遠足や運動会などの学校行事はすでに無く、学校での楽しい思い出はあまりありません。三年生は三階の教室だったので、空襲警報が鳴ると一階まで下りて防空壕へ走らなければなりませんでした。警報が鳴るたびに階段を駆け下りたことだけが思い出されません。

117　岩本光子

ます。

家は学校から子どもの足で十五分ぐらいの八幡神社の近くでした。校舎の裏を通って集団登校するのですが、裏道は木の根が張り、雨が降るとすぐに泥道となって歩きにくいのです。やっと校舎にたどり着いても上階の教室の窓から見ている上級生から、「手の振りや足並みがそろっていなかった」と言われては、隊列行進を最初からやり直させられるのには閉口しました。

その日は、夏休みだったので、家の近くで仲良しの隣家の姉妹と遊んでいました。飛行機が飛んできたので見上げると、黒い物体を落としたのが分かりました。その瞬間、ピカッと凄い光が走り、私たちは爆風に吹き飛ばされたのです。

大きな梅の木が倒れてきて、私は木の根に首を押さえつけられるように

倒れ、右半身には大火傷（やけど）を負っていました。一緒に遊んでいた隣家の姉妹も、木の枝の下敷きになっています。私たち三人は、どうにか梅の木から脱出して、山の方に逃げたのです。

山の中は、逃げてきた人たちでいっぱいだった。腕や胸が赤く焼け爛（ただ）れ、人間とは思えないような姿の人たちがたくさんいた。

岩本さんたち三人は、防空壕へ行ったが人でいっぱい。前の湧水がチョロチョロ流れているところに座り込み、そのまま夜明けを待ったという。

翌朝、姉妹の一人が死亡していた。

原爆により、城山国民学校の在校生の九三％が亡くなったという。

母は三菱製鋼所で被爆し、長与（ながよ）の避難所に逃げましたが、翌日、妹を預けていた叔父のところに迎えに行きました。妹は叔父の養女になることが

岩本光子

決まっていたので、よく預けられていたので叔父の家は無く、無残な瓦礫の山が燻ぶり続け、耐え難い悪臭に満ちていたそうです。母は焼け跡を必死で妹を探しましたが、見つかりませんでした。妹は爆風で飛ばされ、熱線で一瞬にして焼かれたようです。母は、妹の遺骨の代わりに焼け跡の土を容器に詰めて持って来ました。

叔母（母の妹）は、家の前で洗濯物を干していたので、全身に大火傷を負ったが、奇跡的に命だけは助かった。母は近所からリヤカーを借りてきて、全身火傷の叔母を乗せ、リヤカーの隅に岩本さんと従姉妹たちを乗せて新興善小学校の救護所に向かった。

ところが、救護所は足の踏み場もないほど負傷者でいっぱい。でも家は焼けて防空壕で暮らしていたので、そのまま新興善小学校に残ったという。

叔母の火傷はひどく、傷口を這い回るウジ虫を、いつも母が小枝で一つひとつ摘んで取り除いていました。その叔母も亡くなり、母は自分の妹の遺体を一人で焼きました。遺骨を持って戻ってくると、従姉妹の一人が亡くなっており、また、その遺体を焼きに行くことに。

私は、少しは動けるようになったものの、右足はまったく動かず、家の中を這って移動していました。母は、そんな私を背負ってよく按摩に通ってくれました。

硬直した足を揉んでもらうのですが、痛くて泣き叫ぶ私に母は、「ミッコ（光子）、歩けるごとなるとやけん！　我慢せんばよ」と私の身体を押さえつけるのです。だから私は、「あんま」と聞くだけで、震えるほど怖がりました。でもいま、こうやって歩けるようになったのは母のおかげだと、感謝しています。

被爆後、岩本さんは母と五島列島の久賀島の叔父（亡父の兄）のもとに身を寄せた。

島に着いたとき、岩本さんは意識がほとんどなく、死人のようだった。髪はすべて抜け落ち、骨と皮だけにやせ細って、「苦しい、苦しい！」と呻くばかり。あまりの苦しみように、「いっそ早く死んだ方が楽になれるのに」と、皆が話していたという。岩本さんは、「今日死ぬか、明日死ぬか」と思われながら生き続けていたのだ。

寝たきりの私は、赤ちゃんのように母に抱きかかえられなければ、排泄もできませんでした。

ある日、用を済ませ、庭先から母にかかえられて部屋に戻る途中、急に体から「シャーッ」と、流れ出るものがありました。

粗相をしたと思った母は私を叱りましたが、足のつけ根の腫れ上がっていた部分から、膿のようなものが一気に流れ出ていたのでした。
「吸うた原爆のガスが、そこに溜まっていたんだろうね」と、後日、母が語っていました。

その傷口の跡は、いまでも大きく窪んでいます。また、膝と足首にも同様の腫れがあったので、病院で切ってもらい膿を出しました。

そのことがあってから、私は日増しに元気になり、翌年の四月には小学校三年生を、もう一度やり直すことになりました。

久賀島の小学校に入り直したのですが、学校では「彼岸花」という仇名をつけられ、いじめられました。抜け落ちた髪の毛はなかなか生えてこず、やっと生えてきたと思ったら天然パーマで、クルクルと頭の上で踊っていたからです。私も女の子です。本当に傷つき、悲しい思いをしました。

岩本光子

それから間もなく、母は岩本さんを連れて再婚した。義父となったのは、亡くなった叔母（母の妹）の夫だった。彼は妻も三人の娘も亡くし、一人ぼっちだったのだ。

フィリピンから復員して、久賀島の実家に戻った義父に、岩本さんはとても懐いていたそうだ。その様子を見て、「再婚はしない」と言っていた母も、決心したようだった。

私の下に弟妹が四人、生まれました。

ところが、母は野良仕事中に突然、倒れ、福江の病院に運ばれる途中で亡くなったのです。まだ、末の子のお乳も離れていない時期でした。被爆十年目。原爆症でした。

当時、私は十八歳。母の再婚で義理の家族がいるといっても、私は本当

の意味で一人ぼっちになってしまいました。

しかも、義父は壊疽(えそ)に罹(かか)り、働けない身体になっていたのです。

私は四人の幼い弟妹たちの世話から家事一切、そして、母の代わりに野良仕事までやらなくてはならなくなりました。

二人の弟を保育所に預け、三歳の子の手を引き、大きなカゴに乳飲み児と弁当を一緒に入れて背負い、芋畑や田んぼに連れて行きました。三歳児に赤ん坊を見させて、私は苗を植えたり芋の蔓(つる)を起こしたりしました。ミルクも無いので、芋を口の中で柔らかくして乳飲み児に与えるなど、私は文字通り母親代わりでした。

夕方までボロボロになって働き、夜、近所の親類の家に薪(まき)を持って貰い湯に行くことだけが唯一の息抜き、という日々が続きました。

母を慕って泣く弟妹をなだめながら、私の方が泣きたくなったものです。

それに加えて、私と義父の母親との折り合いが悪く、次第に険悪になっ

125　岩本光子

てきました。

長崎に出てきていた父方の叔父が、そんな岩本さんを不憫(ふびん)に思い、長崎に呼んでくれた。岩本さんは心身ともに追いつめられている状態だったため、幼い弟妹たちのことは気がかりだったが義父の母に預け、家を出る決心をした。

ところが、いよいよこれからというときに、被爆とこれまでの無理がたたり、私は強度の貧血症に罹り、原爆病院に通うようになりました。疲れやすく、たびたび、立ちくらみを起こすので、病院へ通うことさえ辛(つら)いほどでした。

結婚適齢期になり、叔父からは縁談話が持ち込まれましたが、「被爆者からは奇形児が生まれる」という話も聞くので、私は、「絶対に結婚はし

ない」と決めていました。

しかし、二十七歳のとき、叔父の強い勧めもあって、電気工事業をしていた主人と結婚したのです。

結婚間もなく、佐賀に住む主人の母が訪ねて来ました。どこからか私のことを聞いたらしく、「原爆におうたん（遭った）だって？」と聞くのです。私は、素直に認めました。

すると、口には出しませんでしたが、義母は、「困った」といった感じで、しかめ面を見せました。

その夜、主人から何か言われるかと思いましたが、何も言われませんでした。義母が主人に言わなかったのか、言ったけれど主人が口にしなかったのかは、分かりません。

だから、そのままにしていました。最後まで、主人には私が被爆者であることは告げなかったのです。

127　岩本光子

最初の子を身ごもったときは、母となる喜びより、生まれてくる子どもへの不安で毎日、苦しみました。

もし奇形児が生まれたら？　戸外で被爆をしたのだから、何もないわけがない……。思いは堂々めぐりしながら、悪い方へ悪い方へと向かうのでした。

夜もよく眠れず、食欲も無くなりましたが、「ともかく五体満足にさえ生まれてくれば！」と、それだけを念じていました。

そして、不安のまま、その日を迎えました。昭和四十年（一九六五）一月、ついに出産したのです。個人病院で、しかも女医さんだったので、出産直後、「手足の指は五本ありますか？　身体に異常はありませんか？」と、私はすがるように尋ねました。

「元気な男の子ですよ」との返事に、胸のつかえがいっぺんに無くなり、何日も悩んでいただけに身体から力が抜けていくようでした。

ところが、それはつかの間の喜びでした。産後八時間ほどして、下半身がヌルヌルしてきたかと思うと、大出血を起こしたのです。
貧血で原爆病院に通っているときは、貧血ばかりに気を取られていましたが、このとき、「白血病と赤血球が増える出血多量症」と診断されました。
すぐに輸血の準備がなされ、私はチューブをつけられて、そのまま一週間余り入院しました。
嬉しかったのは、そんな状態の私でもお乳が張ったことです。勢いよくお乳を吸ってくれる息子を片腕で抱きながら、出産の歓びを噛み締めました。
最初の出産では、輸血で一命を取り留めたが、それから後の出産でも危機に直面した。

二回目の出産(長女)は、設備の整っている市立病院を選んだが、また しても大量の出血で貧血による危篤状態になったのだ。

それだけに、三回目(次女)の出産では、さらに設備の整った大学病院に入院しました。

ところが、赤ん坊は長く産道にいたため、仮死状態で生まれてきたのです。わが子に申し訳なくて、「私の押し出す力が弱くてごめんね！ 絶対に死なないで！」と、泣きながら詫びました。

看護婦さんが赤ん坊を何度も叩き、やっと産声が上がりました。その声を聞いたときは嬉しくて、嬉しくて、思わずベッドから飛び降りて、わが子を抱こうとしたほどです。

原爆は、とくに女性に対してむごい。被爆者ということで破談になった

り、結婚できなかったり、奇形児が生まれるとの噂に出産を諦めたり、妊娠しても出産まで地獄のような不安な日々を送る。そして、無事出産しても岩本さんのように命がけの出産となる原爆は、生命を宿す母を執拗にいじめ続ける。

「入市被爆」を知らず、被爆直後に爆心地に

福下フサエ さん

ふくした・ふさえ　一九三〇年（昭和五年）九月生まれ。十四歳のとき、爆心地から三キロの水の浦三菱造船所で被爆。その後、加津佐で洋裁を習い、二十歳のときに再び長崎に出て保険会社に入社、定年まで勤めた。三十歳で結婚、二女に恵まれる。八十四歳。長崎市滑石在住。

助かった人も原爆病で苦しみながら亡くなっていった

福下フサエさんは、島原半島にある国民学校高等科を卒業し、地元の加津佐(かづさ)青年学校に入学した。在学中に、青年学校から二人だけ長崎の軍需関係の会社に見習い社員として入社することになり、寮に入った。福下さんは、一日交代で学校と水の浦三菱造船所に通った。製図見習いだったが雑用も多く、十一時頃に隣のビルの食堂に課長の昼ご飯を取りに行くことも、仕事の一つだった。パンともう一品、惣菜(そうざい)を受け取って持って来るのだ。

同期のもう一人は、立神(たてがみ)の兵器製作所に配属されていた。

加津佐から長崎に出てきて四カ月目のことでした。あの日も、私は造船所の事務所の六階にいました。ちょうど、十一時になったので、課長の昼ご飯を取りに行こうと出口に向かって歩きかけたとき、大きな爆発音がし

て二方向の窓ガラスが同時に破れ、私の方に飛んできたのです。いつも、とっさに床に伏せる訓練を受けていたのと、暑いけれど長袖を着るようにしていたので、幸いどこにも怪我はありませんでした。事務所にいた人たちは驚いて、われ先にと防空壕へ逃げました。私も人混みに押されるようにして階段を下り、防空壕へ。ここではガラスや物にぶつかって血だらけの人はいましたが、火傷の人は見ませんでした。

その前日、エレベーターの中で製図課の人が腕を三角巾で吊っていたので、「どうされたんです？」と聞くと、「広島に出張に行っていて新型爆弾にやられた！」と言っていました。あの方は原爆に二度、遭ったことになります。

福下さんは夕方まで会社近くの防空壕の中にいて、「もう大丈夫だろう」ということで外に出てみると、対岸（県庁辺り）は火の海だった。このとき

は、まだ何が起こったのか分からなかったという。

寮は爆心地辺りにあったので、帰ろうとしたが、交通手段がすべて止まっていた。当時、福下さんは造船所のある水の浦から船で大波止まで渡り、そこから駒場町の寮まで市電で通っていたのだった。船も市電も動いていないので、福下さんはとりあえず、稲佐まで歩くことにした。夕方五時頃に出発し、寮の辺りに着いたのは七時過ぎだった。歩き始めて進めば進むほど、倒壊した家屋被害がひどくなり、真っ黒に焦げた死体があちこちに転がっていた。三菱製鋼所の辺りに来たときは空に向かって弓のように曲がってはね上がり、製鋼所の建物電のレールは残骸だけになっていた。

二時間ほどかかって寮にたどり着きましたが、寮は跡形もなく吹き飛ばされて、見渡す限りの焼け野原でした。私たちが到着する前に着いていた

二、三人の人たちも、「この辺りじゃない？」と迷ったというほど、周囲は変わっていたのです。

寮は平屋で、長屋のような建物が十数棟ひとかたまりに建っていて、それぞれ勤めている会社（造船所、兵器製作所等）ごとに住んでいました。若い女性ばかり百〜二百人は入居していたと思います。入居者は、五島列島や島原半島から来た人たちもいれば、女学校の勤労奉仕の報国隊の人たちもいました。この人たちは一日おきに丸尾町の広い学習施設に通い、勉強していました。私もこの人たちと一緒に勉強に通っていました。

一日おきに勉強するといっても、朝はいつもの時間に出勤してから丸尾町に向かうのです。丸尾町でも勉強中に空襲警報が鳴ると、近くの防空壕へ避難するのですが、会社と違い気分的にも余裕があったのか、そのうちに慣れっこになって警報が鳴っても防空壕へは入りませんでした。とくに

夏で暑かったので……。

朝は七時に寮を出て造船所に出勤、夕方には戻ってくる。造船所に夜勤はなかったが、夜勤のある会社の寮もあった。各寮には食事を作る人が通っており、全員が食堂で食べていた。

私の住んでいた島原は、まだ食料事情が良かったので、寮で食べる大豆かすや雑草みたいなものが入っている雑炊は食べるのが苦痛でした。畳敷きの六畳一間に三人で生活し、休日には洗濯物を庭に一斉に干したりしました。寮母さん、寮長さんもいましたが、十数棟の寮のすべてを管理している人たちで、どこに住んでいたのか知りません。

寮跡らしき場所に着いてみると、十数棟あった寮はすべて跡形もなく、周りにあった立ち木までがきれいに焼けてなくなっていました。城山国民

学校と山の方の鎮西学院中学校が見えたので、それを目印に寮のあった場所がかろうじて確認できました。

私たち同様、兵器製作所などに勤めていた人たちも、次々と自分たちの寮跡に帰ってきましたが、誰も言葉も出ませんでした。

寮長さん、寮母さんの二人とも、その場で椅子に座ったままの姿で白骨化していたと、後になってから聞きました。夜勤で寮に残っていた人たちも一瞬のうちに全員、亡くなったそうです。

呆然と立っていると、三菱の「係長」の腕章を付けた人に、「ここは危険だから時津の方に避難しなさい」と言われました。長崎に出てきて四カ月の私は、時津がどこにあるのか分かりません。そこにいた十数人の中で知っている人がいたので、その人について歩き出しました。

駒場町の隣の大橋まで来ると、橋は吹き飛ばされ剝きだしの鉄骨だけが残っており、這うようにして渡りました。下を見ると、水を求めて川にた

どり着いた負傷者が呻き声をあげ、助けを求めています。川にはまったり、流されたりしていました。

三菱製鋼所の辺りで見た被爆者はすでに死体になっていたので、諦めに似た気持ちになり、それほど気にはならなかったのですが、ここでは人々が悲鳴を上げ必死にもがいているので、かわいそうでたまりませんでした。でも、私たちではどうすることもできず、黙って時津に向かって歩くだけでした。

深夜になって、やっと時津に到着。昼からなにも食べていなかったので、村の人たちがくれた炊き出しのおむすびが、とてもおいしかったことを覚えています。その夜は大きな家に泊めてもらい、蚊帳の中でごろ寝できたときはやっと安心しました。

翌日、「島原方面の人は家に帰るように」と言われ、道の尾駅まで行くと駅裏の広場には怪我人が大勢おり、しかもまだ続々と集まってくるよう

139 福下フサエ

でした。
　服がちぎれて血で染まった人、被ったヘルメットの形だけ髪の毛が残り、耳や首など露出している部分がすべて焼け爛れている人など、目を背けたくなるほどでした。
　頼んで汽車に乗せてもらいましたが、その日には着くことができず、島原駅で一晩、列車の中に泊まり、加津佐のわが家には翌日に着きました。
　母は、「フサエはとうに死んでいるだろう」「フサエの死体をどうやって探せばいいんだろうか」と家族で話し合っていました。聞けば、加津佐からキノコ雲が見え、長崎の町が一晩中燃えているのが見えたということです。
　友だちも亡くなり、助かった人もその後、原爆症で苦しみながら亡くなっていきました。また、いつ発症するか不安の日々を過ごしている人も

私はその後、加津佐で洋裁を習ったりしましたが、二十歳のときに友だちに誘われて再び長崎に出てきて保険会社に勤め、それから二十六年間、定年まで勤めました。

三十歳のときに、知人の紹介で青果会社に勤めていた熊本県出身の主人と結婚。私より十歳も年上で、とても大事にしてくれました。

長女を妊娠したとき、私も少し不安になりましたが、主人が「足の指の長い児が生まれたりせんかな。五体満足な子が生まれてほしいな」と言ったので、「ああ、少しは被爆の影響を気にしていたんだな」と、思いました。

娘が二人いますが、長女が小学校のとき健康診断で、医師から「少し貧血気味ですね」と言われたことがありました。普段は気にしていなくても、

何かあると「もしかしたら?」と思ってしまう。それが嫌です。
放射能の影響なんて、あの当時はまったく知りませんでした。だから、被爆直後に私たちは爆心地の駒場町（いまの松山町付近）の寮跡に行ったのです。

後から、片づけのために爆心地に入った兵隊が原因不明の病気で大学病院に入院したり、亡くなったりしたというのを聞いて、初めて「入市被爆」ということを知ったのです。

これをどう理解していいのか分かりません。ですから、「放射能の効力は直後には出てこないで、ある程度、時間が経ってから出てくる。被爆直後に爆心地に入った私たちのときはまだ放射能ガスは出ていなかった」と思っています。科学的にどうかは知りませんが、そうでも結論づけなければ、とてもやりきれないのです。

城山国民学校千五百人の児童が百人に

森本正記 さん

もりもと・まさき 一九三三年(昭和八年)四月生まれ。十二歳のとき、爆心地から一・二キロ離れた城山町の溜め池で遊んでいて被爆。城山国民学校の約千五百人の児童は百人足らずしか生き残らなかった。八十二歳。長崎市柳谷町在住。

亡くなった同窓生のためにも被爆体験を語り継ぎたい

あの日、城山国民学校六年だった森本正記さんは朝九時頃から、近所の友だち十人と近くの溜め池に泳ぎに行った。朝から蒸し暑く、みんな六尺ふんどしで泳いでいた。

私たちは夢中で泳ぎ、くたびれたし腹も減ったので帰ろうと思いました。シャツとズボンを穿き、二、三人で土手に上がりかけたとき、五年生の子が空を指さして、
「ああ、落下傘爆弾だぞ！ みんな見らんか！」
と叫びました。他の子どもたちも、
「どらどら？」
と、水から上がり土手を駆け登りました。傘が三つに重なった奇怪なパ

森本正記

ラシュートが長崎造船所上空から風に乗って近づいてきて、木々の生い茂っている辺りまで来たときです。

辺り一面、真っ白になったかと思うと、私はそのまま何も分からなくなりました。まるで白い雲の中にいるようでした。

気がつくと、私は溜め池の水の中にいました。吹き飛ばされて土手を転げ落ち、池に落ちたらしいのです。

私の場合、水に落ちたことが幸いしました。水に浸かった部分は火傷を免れ、とっさに顔を伏せたので顔は何ともありませんでした。しかし、頭、腹、手足に火傷を負いました。

胸が熱いので手を当ててみると、手が肌に付き、ペロッと胸の皮が剥けました。衣服はボロボロに焦げ、腕の皮はほとんど剥けている状態でした。後で聞いたところ、土手を見ると、十人いた友だちが二、三人しかいません。後で聞いたところ、そのなかの七人が一週間も経たずに次々と亡くなったということで

森本さんは、溜め池から城山の家まで一人で、よろけるようにして戻った。上から踏み潰されたようにペチャンコになった家が、累々と続いていた。周りは飛び散った瓦礫(がれき)で足の踏み場もないほどで、地面を歩いているのか潰れた屋根の上を歩いているのかさえ、分からなかった。

やっと、わが家に着いたのですが、家は爆風で吹き飛ばされ、潰れて中に入ることもできません。私は呆然(ぼうぜん)と家の前に立ち尽くしたまま、体から力が抜けていくのを感じていました。

かろうじて動ける人たちは、わが家の近くの防空壕へ避難していました。私も防空壕に向かって歩き出しましたが、裸足(はだし)でしたので、途中で急に歩かれんようになりました。見ると、右足の親指の付け根がザックリと裂け、

親指がプランプランとちぎれそうになっていたのです。私は足の指を押さえ、這うにして防空壕にたどり着きました。這ってくる人、背負われてくる人、抱きかかえられて避難してくる人、被爆者は悲惨な状態でした。

眼球が飛び出し、目のところが大きな穴になったままの人もいました。その人はその後、傷口にウジが湧き、くり抜かれた目玉の穴の奥で何匹ものウジが蠢いていました。

体中にガラスが突き刺さり、周りの人も手が付けられない状態の人もいました。臭いと呻き声で耐えられず、防空壕の前に水の枯れた小川があったので、私はそこに這って行き、二日間、横になっていました。

やがて、父が探しに来て、私を見るなり、

「畑に来いと言っとるのに何で来んかったとか」

と怒りました。

148

というのは、当時、父は山奥の土地を開墾して芋を植えていて、私も前日は手伝いに行ったのですが、この日は友だちが誘いに来たので泳ぎに行ってしまったのです。

母は、潰れた家の梁で頭を打って気を失っていたということを、私は後で知りました。

父は、壊れた家の使えそうな柱や梁を家の前の木に立てかけ、その下の三畳間ほどの空間に畳を敷いて私を寝かせてくれました。火傷が化膿し、傷口からジュクジュクと膿が流れていました。

とくに蜂の多い夏で、それを蜂が吸いに来るのです。膿を吸っている蜂を追い払うと、刺して逃げるのですが、これが結構、痛いのです。だから、蜂もハエも追い払えません。

私は生ける屍そのもの。まったく、惨めでした。

足の親指の傷は、芋の蔓草を揉んでつける程度の治療でしっかりと、

149　森本正記

くっつきましたが、胸から腹にかけての火傷は、なかなか治りませんでした。

一週間ほど経って、城山国民学校の広場に救護所ができたので、森本さんは父に背負われて行った。やっと、油のようなものを塗るという、手当てらしいことをしてもらった。包帯代わりに大きな三角巾を腹掛けのように当て、背中で結んだ。

これが大変でした。血膿で三角巾が固まり、傷口にベッタリ張り付いて剥がれないのです。端から水を浸けて三日がかりで剥がしたら、胸から腹にかけてツルリと皮が剥けてしまいました。真っ赤な、剥きだしの皮膚から汁が出るのですが、以後は何もせずに自然乾燥させることにしました。

でも、不思議なことに、苦しいとか、悲しいとかは感じなかったのです。

友だちの死体を見ても何とも思わなくなっていました。神経が麻痺していたのでしょう。

いつまでも外と変わらない三畳ほどの地べたに寝かせておくのもかわいそうということで、森本さんは一時、父の実家の川原町に移された。姉である長女と次女が、すでに川原町の叔父（父の弟）のところに世話になっており、森本さんも、そこに運ばれた。二カ月後、大工仕事もできる父が、潰れた家の廃材を集めて六畳二間のバラック小屋を建てたので、そちらに移った。

この頃、胸、腹の火傷ばかりではなく、慢性の下痢が続き、髪の毛も抜け出したのです。
父は、「大切に飲めよ」と、五十円分（現在の五万〜十万円程度）の漢方薬

を買ってきて飲ませてくれました。苦くて飲みにくい薬でしたが、驚異的な効き目でした。高価な薬なので一日一回の服用でしたが、まず下痢と抜け毛が止まり意識もハッキリしてきました。塗り薬もつけていないのに、胸と腹もみるみるかさぶた状になり、快方に向かっていきました。でも、亀の腹のような、かさぶただらけの胸と腹は痒くて、痒くて、たまりませんでした。

この年の十一月にはかさぶたもほとんどとれ、授業再開の知らせを受けた私は登校しました。行ってみると、同級生のほとんどが亡くなっていました。千五百人近くいた城山国民学校の児童は、百人足らずしか生き残っていなかったのです。

私たちは、三キロほど離れた稲佐国民学校の一室を借りて授業を受けました。翌年の春、私たち六年生は卒業しました。全部で十四人でした。

卒業した年の夏、川原町の叔父のところに世話になっていた長姉が原爆

症で亡くなりました。

また、昭和二十六年（一九五一）には、外傷のなかった次女も白血病で亡くなりました。

被爆から二十三年後の昭和四十三年（一九六八）、第一回の城山国民学校同窓会が某テレビ局の企画で開催されました。十四人いた同窓生は九人になっていました。その後も、毎年、何人かが亡くなっていき、いまではほとんど残っていません。

城山国民学校の思い出といっても、夏休みの前から授業をやっていなかったし、ほとんど休みだったので、あまりありません。

ただ、運動場が畑になっていて、豆や芋が植えてあったことだけは鮮明に覚えています。

森本正記

森本さんは、十七歳のときに近所の人の紹介で長崎市の土木課に就職した。職員として三十年間勤め、その後、本庁の守衛に異動、十四年働いた。職員として四十四年間勤めたことになる。

その間、昭和三十二年（一九五七）に結婚。二歳年上の妻は布津町出身。その後、娘二人を授かり幸せな結婚生活をおくる。七十三歳のときに前立腺がんを患ったが、それも乗り越えた。

長女が小さい頃、休日になると娘をおぶった妻をオートバイの後ろに乗せ、町まで出かけたことが楽しい思い出です。

溜め池にいたので、真っ先に死んでもおかしくない私がこうして生きている。このことに感謝し、亡くなった城山国民学校の同窓生のためにも被爆体験を語り継いでいこうと思います。

苦しさも悲しさも
和歌に託して耐えた母

田﨑弥寿子 さん

たさき・やすこ　一九四五年(昭和二十年)十一月生まれ。爆心地から三キロの西山町の自宅で被爆(七カ月目の胎内被爆)。子どものころ、両親が離婚。結核で療養中の母と文通したことを機に、文章を書くことが好きになり、作文で数々の賞を受ける。小児結核の再発から腎臓結核を患った。二十七歳で結婚。六十九歳。諫早市永昌東町在住。

病気の母と別れた父への不信感は再会したことで払拭された

　私は、胎内被爆児です。私の被爆者手帳を見ると、「被爆時の年齢—胎児」「被爆場所—長崎市下西山町（爆心地から三キロメートル）」「被爆直後の状況—岩川町（被爆地から一キロメートル）に外出中の曽祖父を見つけに入った（母体中）」と、記されています。

　母（国武縫子）は当時、二十歳。私は母の胎内で七カ月目でした。

　あの日、空襲警報が解除になり、母はお姑さんとおしゃべりしながら、生まれてくる私の産着を縫っていたそうです。

　「一瞬、稲妻のような閃光が走ったかと思うと、続いてもの凄い轟音がして、箪笥や周囲の家具、天井の梁が倒れ落ちてきた。母は本能的にお腹の

田﨑弥寿子

子をかばい、うつ伏せになった」ということを、田﨑さんは後で聞いたという。

あの騒動のなかで、「長崎市内に住んでいる母方の曽祖父の行方が分からない」との連絡があり、翌日、田﨑さんの母はお姑さんと二人で曽祖父を探しに出た。母は大きなお腹をかかえて諏訪神社近くの家から爆心地を通り抜け、岩川町の親類の家を訪ねた。「放射能」という言葉さえ知らない母たちは、自ら爆心地に入っていったのだ。

その後、幸い、曽祖父は無事に戻ってきたのですが、直後から身体の不調を訴え、翌年六月に原因不明の病で亡くなりました。

健康優良児で、小学校から女学校卒業まで一日も学校を休んだことがなかったという母は、私を出産してから日増しに病弱になり、昭和二十三年(一九四八)一月に弟を出産した頃には、極度の貧血、心臓病、低血圧に苦

しみ、肺結核を患うようになってしまいました。
そして、長期治療のため、田上(たがみ)の結核療養所に入院することになりました。

生まれたばかりの弟は、跡取りということで父方へ引き取られ、三歳に満たない私は、諫早(いさはや)に住む母の祖父母のところへ引き取られました。幼い私たち姉弟は、それっきり別々の人生を歩むことになったのです。
私は父親の顔を知らずに育ちました。物心ついたときには、母はすでに療養所生活でした。そして、いつの間にか両親は離婚していたのです。
私と母の間で、父のことが話題になったことはありません。母も話しませんでしたし、私も聞きませんでした。
でも、私の胸の奥には、ずっと「病む母と離婚した父親」への不信感がありました。

159　田﨑弥寿子

私もまた、健康体ではなく、疲れやすく貧血で倒れることがたびたびありました。朝礼が少しでも長引くと、目の前が真っ暗になって座り込むというありさまです。体育や運動会はいつも見学。その後、小児結核に罹（かか）り、毎日、お尻にストレプトマイシンの注射を打ちました。学校は一年、休学しました。
　月に一度、諫早から祖父に連れられて、バスで長崎の母に会いに行くのが、私の唯一の楽しみでした。バス停から小高い丘の上の療養所までの長い坂を登って行くのですが、「もうすぐ母に会える」と思うと嬉（うれ）しくて、嬉しくて、胸が弾みました。
　母の病室は、女性患者だけの六人部屋でした。療養所の林の中を、私は母とよく散歩したものです。
　また、私は学校で習った、知っている限りの歌を母に歌って聞かせまし

あるとき、母が、「私が音痴だから、やっぱりあんたも音痴ね」と、笑いながら言ったことがありました。でも、私にはそれが少しも嫌なことではなく、むしろ母と似ていることが嬉しかったのです。

田上の療養所の敷地内には、ひときわ大きくて不気味な建物があった。それは火葬場だった。伝染を恐れ、亡くなった患者は療養所内で火葬にしていたのだ。

祖母は私の頭を撫でながら、「原爆さえ、戦争さえ、なかったら……。あんな病気にさえ、ならなかったら、こんなにもかわいそうな母子にならずに済んだのに」と、よく涙ぐんでいました。

あれほど楽しみだった母との面会も、私や母の体調不良で行けなくなる

ことがしばしばありました。

そんなとき、私は母に手紙を書きました。友だちのこと、祖父母のこと、思いついたことなどを次々と書き綴り、母に送ったのです。

すると、母は私の手紙を添削して送り返してくれました。それが嬉しくて、何度も何度も手紙を書き、作文や読書感想文等も同封して送りました。母との文通は、私に書くことの楽しさを教えてくれました。その甲斐あってか、私は作文大会で何度も賞をいただきました。

昭和三十五年頃、田﨑さんの母は、片方の肺を肋骨ごと全部取ってしまうという、画期的な手術を受けることを決意する。「生存率六割」という手術を、「賭ける」思いで受けたのだった。翌年、母は十二年間の療養生活から生還してきたのである。

信じられないことでした。諫早の祖父母の家で、初めて母と寝た夜のことは、いまでも忘れられません。中学生だった私は、すでに母と同じ背丈になっていました。母と布団を並べて、いつまでも話していました。

高校を卒業し、地元の銀行に勤めるようになって数年後の二十二歳のとき、小児結核が再発して腎臓結核になり、私は腎臓を一つ摘出しました。銀行も退職しました。

昭和四十七年（一九七二）、二十七歳のときに主人と知り合い、結婚することになりました。

ところが祖父が大反対。「弥寿子は一人娘なのだから養子をとって『国武の家』を継ぐように！」と、養子を探し始めたのです。

そのとき、母は、「結婚は好きになった人としなさい」と、私の背中を押してくれました。

田﨑弥寿子

翌年、私が二歳のときに別れた弟の「結婚の知らせ」が届きました。父は再婚しており、その再婚相手の方が、「結婚する前に一度会っては」と、知らせてくれたのです。

母は、「育ててこなかった私が、いまさら会うのは申し訳ない」と、拒みましたが、「いま会わなければ、もう一生会えないのよ」と、私は説得し、会うことになりました。弟は当時、名古屋に住んでいました。祖父の病気見舞いを理由に、長崎の病院で会ったのですが、私はそのときの母の様子や弟の態度は、なぜか何も覚えていません。ただ、初めて会ったのに「実の弟だ！」と実感したことだけは、確かに覚えているのです。

母が弟と会ったのは、この一回きりだった。次に弟が母と会ったのは、

「母の葬儀」のときだったからだ。

「あのとき、無理しても会わせてあげてよかった」と、田﨑さんは思ったという。母の葬儀には、父も駆けつけてくれた。そこで、田﨑さんは、父と母が六歳違いだったことなどを知った。

また、弟と会ったことで、いろいろなことが分かった。母と別れた父は、「姉と弟が同じ長崎にいるのはよくないだろう」と、船舶関係の仕事をしていたツテで横浜に引っ越し、再婚したのだった。

母は療養中に和歌を詠むようになり、滑らかな文字で書かれた和歌集をたくさん遺していました。

母の死後、遺された日記や和歌を初めて読んだとき、父が母のもとを去ったのではなく、母の方から離婚を申し出て、強引に実行したことが分かったのです。母の句によって……。

「ベッドより宙に揉まるる雪見つつ　みずから去りし妻の座思う」

終戦当時、肺結核は不治の病ともいわれ、伝染することで最も世間に恐れられていた病気でした。

そして、何よりも栄養を取らなければならない病でもあったため、肺結核の患者が出ると、その家はお金がいくらあっても足らないといわれていたのです。

父は財産を処分してでも母に栄養のあるものを、と懸命だったそうです。母は自分の病が長期療養になることを察して、父の好意を断り離婚を決意したのでした。自分の病気で父の一生を狂わせたくないと思ったのでしょう。

それは、当時、決して治ることはないという病に罹った母の、父に対し

ての精いっぱいの誠意だったのではないでしょうか。

「買いおきし口紅ひかむ枕辺に　別れし夫の便り来し朝」

母はベッドの中で声を殺して泣いた夜もあったはずです。どんなにか、自分の病を恨めしく思ったことでしょう。でも、自分から望んだ離婚を後悔はしていなかったと思います。

やがて、母の最期が訪れました。昭和五十三年（一九七八）五月中旬、母は私が淹れたお茶をおいしそうに啜りながら、「ヤッちゃん、お母さん少し疲れたみたい。明日から二、三日、入院してみるけん」と言い、翌日、かかりつけの病院へ入院しました。

五月三十日の夕方、母が珍しく「スイカが食べたい」と言うのです。普

田﨑弥寿子

段、何かをねだるということのない母だったので、スイカの季節ではありませんでしたが、私は探しに行きました。
やっと見つけたスイカを母のところへ持っていくと、無邪気に喜び、ひとくち口に含んで、「まだ少し早かね。あまりおいしくない」と、少し顔をしかめました。それでも、一切れ食べてくれたので、私はほっとしました。
病室を出るとき、「明日ね！」と私が声をかけると、母は「おやすみ」と言って、ドアのところで振り返った私に、ニッコリして手を挙げました。
それが、生きている母の最後の姿でした。

　久々に　故郷帰りし
　子や孫の　しぐさに見つけた
　母の面影
　　　　弥寿子

母の遺骨もなく、亡くなったとは信じられない

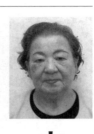

山口テル子 さん

やまぐち・てるこ 一九二八年（昭和三年）十月生まれ。爆心地から一・八キロの住吉神社下の自宅で被爆。母は知人の家で亡くなり、父は背中に大火傷を負う。弟は背中にガラス片が突き刺さった。両親が以前、経営していたクリーニング店を、戦後、きょうだい四人で再開させる。十八歳で結婚し、六人の子どもに恵まれた。八十六歳。長崎市平和町在住。

痒くてたまらないという父の火傷の跡を子どもたちが一晩中さすった

山口さんの両親は、岩川町でクリーニング店を営んでいた。戦争が激しさを増し、食料が配給制になると、両親は住吉神社下の畑付きの一軒家を購入。店を山口さんらに任せ、食料を確保するために田んぼや畑で稲や芋を作った。店は、当時十六歳の山口さんと、すぐ上の姉、職人さんの三人で切り盛りしていた。

山口さんは、男四人、女五人きょうだいの七番目だった。次兄と三兄はビルマの戦地に赴いており、次姉は上海に嫁いでいた。住吉神社下の家には、両親と、ほかのきょうだい、長姉の子ども二人、従兄弟（母の亡くなった妹の子ども）二人が住む大家族だった。

八月一日に激しい空襲があり、これ以上、クリーニング店を続けるのは

危険だということで、山口さんと姉は、その家に荷物を運び込むことになり、八月初旬から大八車で少しずつ荷物を運び出していた。

八月九日も、荷物の運び出しの続きをする予定になっていましたが、私たちは疲れてしまい、先に運んでおいた衣類の虫干しをすることにしました。

あのとき、私は昼ご飯の支度をするため、台所でじゃが芋の皮を剥いていました。

高校生と小学六年生の従兄弟が、「叔母ちゃん、落下傘が落ちよるよ!」と言うので、「落下傘ならふんわり落ちるだろうから」と、じゃが芋の残り半分の皮を剥き、終わって外へ出ようとしたその瞬間、硫黄のような臭いと青い煙が「モワ〜ン」と入ってきたのです。あわてて家の中に引っ込み、土間の釣瓶井戸の端につかまりました。

音も光も感じませんでした。

一瞬、何が起こったのか分からないくらいの衝撃があり、周囲を見渡すとガラス戸は破れ、家の中がメチャクチャになっていたのです。

腰が抜けたようになって立ち上がることができず、這うようにして外へ出てみると、そこにあったのは先ほど声を掛けてくれた二人の従兄弟の無残な姿でした。

着ていた衣類は焼けて半裸。顔、腕など肌が出ているところは焼け爛れ、皮が一枚ペロリと剝けて赤い肉が剝き出しになっています。

消防隊員が「火傷の者に水を飲ませるな！」と声を掛けて回っていた。二人を家の中に入れ、寝かせようとしましたが、全身火傷のため、横にさせることもできません。土間に腰かけさせ、手当てをしようとすると、二人はしきりに「水が飲みたい！」と言うのです。水を飲ませるといけな

山口テル子

いので畑の種キュウリを取ってきて皮を剝いてやりました。あのとき、しまいまでじゃが芋の皮を剝かずに外に飛び出していたら、私も従兄弟たちと同じ状態になっていたはずです。それよりも、前日同様に荷物の運び出しをしていたら、爆心地から五百メートルと離れていない岩川町にいた私たちは、間違いなく即死でした。

従兄弟たちは結局、我慢ができなくて夜中に井戸の水をたっぷり飲んでしまったらしく、翌朝、二人は水ぶくれのように顔も身体もパンパンに腫れ上がっていました。

数日後、長姉夫婦が従兄弟たちを道の尾小学校の救護所に連れて行きましたが、八月十一日に下の子が、八月十七日に上の子が亡くなりました。

父も、従兄弟たち同様、戸外にいて爆風で一間半も飛ばされ、ナス畑に倒れていました。背中を丸めて、家の前の畑の草むしりをしていたので、背中に大火傷を負いました。

住吉神社付近は茅葺き屋根が多かったため、火は物置小屋から母屋に燃え移り、辺りに次々と燃え広がっていった。

山口さんらが引っ越した家は、物置小屋も母屋も屋根は瓦葺きだったのと近所と離れていたため燃えなかった。焼け残ったのはその家、一軒だけだったのだ。だが、家の中がめちゃくちゃになっていたので、山口さんたちは防空壕に向かった。

火傷と死体の強烈な臭いで、私たちは防空壕の中に入ることができませんでした。防空壕の中で、無事だった人たちが抱き合い、泣いて喜んでいるのが見えました。家族が行方不明になった人たちが大声で子どもや肉親を探して呼ぶ声もまた、聞こえていました。

翌日、おにぎりが配給になりましたが、食欲が出るはずもなく、食べて

いる人はほとんどいませんでした。

弟は長崎商業学校に通っていましたが、すでに授業はなく、教室は兵器製作工場に使われていました。弟はその作業を手伝っていて被爆。日頃の訓練のおかげで、とっさに床に伏せましたが、爆風とともに工場のガラスが落ちてきて背中に無数に突き刺さりました。隣にいた同級生は間に合わず、腹が破裂して即死したといいます。

工場で手当てを受けた弟は、電車道を歩き通し、包帯姿でわが家に到着。途中、火傷を負った被爆者たちが口々に「水くれ！　水！」と手を伸ばし、弟の足首にしがみ付くので、「水を汲んでくるから手を離してくれ」と言って逃げてきたそうです。

父と弟は、島原の池田病院に治療に行きました。島原へ行く途中、キュウリを貼った父の首、背中、足の火傷の傷口には何百匹もの白いウジが湧

いていたそうです。父と弟は病院の前の民家を借りて、治療に専念しました。

母はあの日、「八月一日の空襲」で、岩川町のわが家がどうなったか気になり、わが家を見に行くついでに、「山王神社近くの近藤さんのところに寄るから」と、畑のナスやキュウリを持って出かけたまま、行方不明になっていました。母の消息が分かったのは九月に入ってからでした。

三菱兵器製作所の工場で働いていた近藤さんのご主人は、原爆投下の直後、自宅に駆けつけたところ、崩れた家の下敷きになった末の娘（五歳）を発見。いくら引っ張り出そうとしても瓦礫（がれき）の中からその子を引きだすことができなかった。そのとき、「ここには誰がいたと？」と聞いたところ、「兄ちゃんと姉ちゃんと私。それと、母ちゃんと井上さんのおばちゃん（山

口さんの母）がいた」と答えたという。山口さんは、後になってそのことを聞き、近藤さんの家で母が亡くなったことを知ったのだった。

母の遺骨もなく、遺体も見ていないので、いつまで経っても諦めきれず、夜に足音が聞こえたりすると、「母が戻ってきたのではないか」と何度も起きました。

何年経っても戻ってこないところを見ると、「近藤さんのお宅で亡くなったのかなあ」と、諦めざるを得ませんでした。

一人残った近藤さんのご主人は、その後、精神のバランスを崩し、亡くなったそうです。

原爆投下の半月後、危機一髪で助かった私を、大阪から叔母たち二人が見舞いに来てくれました。火事を免れたものの、家もかなり傾いており、

「どうぞ、中に入って休んでください」と言っても、叔母たちは怖がって入ろうとしません。

私は冷たい麦茶をお盆にのせて、外に立ったままの叔母たちの前に持って行きました。

その瞬間、轟音とともに家が崩れ落ちたのです。叔母たちと顔を見合わせたまま、私は歯の根も合わないほどブルブル震えました。

家が潰れたので、私と妹は北有馬（島原）の叔母の家で、他の兄弟は父と弟が治療のため借りている家で生活することになりました。

父の背中は傷口が固まり、火傷の跡が両手の指を伸ばしたような太さで盛り上がっていました。夜になって身体が温かくなると痒くて我慢できないらしく、私たち子どもが交代で一晩中さすりました。

住吉神社下の家の近所の人たちが島原まで訪ねてきて、潰れて住めなくなった家の柱や梁を売ってほしいと言うので承諾すると、家はみるみる原

形を留めないほど変わり果てました。

被爆の年の秋、再び住吉神社下の近所の人たちが訪ねてきました。うちの田んぼの稲が実っているので、その米を分けてほしいというのです。田んぼに行ってみると、世話をする人もいないのに、春に父母が植えた稲がたわわに実っていました。刈り取ってみると、十三俵もの収穫がありました。

翌年の三月、私は通学していた女子商業学校の卒業試験を受け、卒業証書を取りに行きました。そこであらためて、多くの同級生が亡くなったことを知りました。

島原から戻ると、私と長兄、すぐ上の三姉、兵隊から帰ってきた三兄の四人で眼鏡橋のところで「井上クリーニング店」を再開しました。

そして、私は十八歳のときに、長兄の紹介で同業の主人と結婚。二年後

に独立して、平和町で夫婦でクリーニング店を開業しました。その後、六人の子どもに恵まれました。

父の火傷は治りましたが結核を患い、昭和二十六年（一九五一）の元旦、亡くなりました。

私も、最初は極度の貧血でちょくちょく倒れましたが、いまはずいぶん良くなっています。

ガラスが刺さり、ハリネズミのようになった弟は、いまだに「なんやら痛い！　ガサガサする」と言っては病院でその部分を切開しています。すると、ガラスの破片が出てきて、これを取り除くと、跡がイボのようになります。弟の背中はイボだらけでした。

原爆で受けた心と身体の傷は、いつまでも消えることはありません。

181　山口テル子

被爆死した同胞たちへの祈りをこめ、チマチョゴリで平和式典に参列

権 舜琴 さん

クォン・スングン　一九二六年（昭和元年）一月、韓国・安東市生まれ。爆心地から一・八キロの旭町で被爆。夫と建設工事現場の宿舎や古鉄商を営み、後に焼肉店を開業。三階建ての焼肉ビルにまで拡大する。現在、在日本大韓民国民団婦人会長崎本部常任顧問。故・夫は民団（現・在日本大韓民国民団）の長崎県地方本部地方団長、長崎商銀信用組合の理事長を務める。八十九歳。長崎県銅座町在住。

苦労を共にしてきた夫はがんに罹り、「おまえ、先に行くよ」と韓国語で呟いた

　私は四歳のときに母に連れられて、先に渡日していた父のいる京都に来ました。若いときの父はいい加減な人で、すぐにフラリとどこかへ行ってしまいます。そのたびに、母と一緒に父を追って四日市、岐阜、名古屋、佐世保と、日本中を転々としました。

　京都には小学校四年生までいました。米が買えないほどの貧乏で、おにぎりを作ってもらえないので、遠足にも行けませんでした。

　小学校では「ニンニク臭い！」「朝鮮人！」と馬鹿にされました。雨の日に、傘をさして迎えに来たチマチョゴリの母を見て、友だちに馬鹿にされるのを恐れ、私は母を避けて帰りました。家に帰って母に謝りましたが、そのときに、「この服（チマチョゴリ）しか持っていないからねえ」

と言った、母の悲しそうな顔は忘れられません。

私が十五歳のとき、長崎・佐世保に引っ越してきました。この年に妹が生まれました。

私は佐世保の相浦高等小学校に通っていましたが、身体の弱かった母は私に、「学校に妹をからって（背負って）いけ」と言うのです。

授業中に妹が泣くと、私は教室を出て廊下で妹をあやしました。そこを通っていく子どもたちが「やらしか、やらしか」と言います。言葉の分からない私は、ずっと、「汚い」とか「いやらしい」など、馬鹿にした言葉だと思っていました。それが、「かわいいね」という長崎弁だったことを、後で知りました。

父は朝鮮半島に渡って日本で働きたい労働者を集め、長崎で飯場（現場

（宿舎）の経営を始めました。トタン屋根のバラック小屋には、五、六人の独身の作業員が寝泊まりしていました。

私は、本当は勉強して看護婦さんになりたかったのですが、学校を辞めて、その人たちの食事の支度などを手伝うことになりました。

父の仕事の現場は、主に香焼島にありました。香焼島・本村には当時、強制連行されてきた朝鮮の人たちがずいぶんいて、徹夜の突貫工事など、きつい仕事をさせられていました。私はその人たちと一緒になって働きました。

私にとっても、香焼島は大変なところでした。島には水が無いので、長崎から船で水を運ばなければなりません。島に着いた船から、天秤棒の両端に一斗缶を吊るして何度も水を運ぶのが炊事係の私の仕事で、十五歳の

身体には、こたえるものでした。

父の下で事務に携わっていたチョ・ヨンシクという、私より十一歳上の男性と、十八歳のときに結婚し、香焼島で所帯を持ちました。後年、夫は私に、「おまえの背が低いのは、伸び盛りに重い水汲みをしたからだな」としみじみと言ったことがあります。

夫はその後、父の会社から独立。父は仕事が終わるとお酒を飲むのが楽しみだったのですが、夫は一滴も飲まない人でした。そんなこともあって、夫は九人の人夫を連れて小瀬戸で飯場を立ち上げたのです。

その頃から、空襲はひどくなった。町のあちこちで壊れた家の修復が行われたので、仕事はいくらでもあったという。夫は小瀬戸、西泊など四、五カ所の飯場を持つまでになり、人夫も三十人余りに増えた。子どもも い

なかったので、権舜琴さんは、夫と共に飯場を回りながら人夫の世話をした。

八月九日のあの日、私はお昼の支度をするために旭町の稲佐橋詰所に戻ってきました。夫も入れ違いに戻ってきたので、お茶を出そうとした瞬間、「バーン」と凄い音がしたのです。外に出てみると黒煙が、みるみるうちに空全体に広がっていき真っ暗になりました。詰所の前を、焼け爛れた人たちの群れがゾロゾロと歩いていきます。たちまち町のあちこちで火災が起こり、浦上川には馬や牛だけでなく、人間の死体が無数に浮いていました。

交通手段も無く、権舜琴さんは夫と山越えして、小瀬戸まで歩いて帰ってきた。

翌日、夫は爆心地の松山町をはじめ、各飯場を回ったが、飯場は爆風で跡形も無くなり、人夫は一人もいなかった。焼け死んで瓦礫(がれき)の下に埋まったのか、逃げてしまったのかは分からなかった。三十余人いた人夫のうち、消息が分かったのは作業現場に向かうため大波止から市営船に乗っていて亡くなった二人だけという。

夫は毎日、各飯場跡を回り、うちの人夫を探しましたが、最後まで見つかりませんでした。

長崎には当時、七万人の朝鮮人がいたといいます。うち二万人が被爆し、一万人が死亡したといわれています。その中には、強制連行された朝鮮人労働者もずいぶんいたと思います。

その後の同胞の状況は悲惨でした。被爆を生き延びた人たちで、行き先のある人はほとんどいません。わが家に、「食べ物をください」と、たく

さんの同胞が来ました。

春雨橋の辺りでは、強制労働者も含めて頼っていくところのない同胞が、農家の畑の大根を抜いてきて売ったり、芋を貰ってきて売ったりしていました。春雨橋付近は、みるみるバラック建ての"朝鮮人部落"になりました。日本の男性は兵隊に行って少なかったためか、同胞と仲良くなって一緒に住むようになった日本女性を、橋の周りで多く見かけました。

わが家も大変でした。夫は建設共同組合から下請けの仕事を貰って、ずっと一人で被爆地の後片づけの仕事をしていました。

両親は終戦後、十月頃に韓国へ帰りました。

飯場はやっていけず、夫と二人で神戸・三宮から運動靴を仕入れて売ったり、それでも食べていけず、密造酒(マッコリ)を造って売りました。ところが、それが発覚して警察がやってきたのです。夫は大阪に逃げ、

逃げ遅れた私は逮捕されてこっぴどく取り調べられましたが、「知らぬ存ぜぬ」で通しました。最後には、取り調べの警察官に「あんたは凄いね!」と感心されたほどです。

その後、夫が戻ってきたので二人でリヤカーを引いて古鉄商を始め、集めた古鉄をよく佐世保の業者に売りに行った。

昭和三十八年(一九六三)、夫と二人で働き続け、やっと小さな焼肉屋「アリラン亭」を開業。まだ焼肉が日本では知られていない頃のことだ。

この頃、夫は民団(現・在日本大韓民国民団)の長崎県地方本部地方団長を辞めて、長崎商銀信用組合の理事長になったばかりでした。「店(アリラン亭)のことは手伝ってやれんから、おまえの好きなように商売せい!」と言われ、一人で頑張りました。その甲斐あって、三階建ての

焼肉ビルにまで広げ、三階の大広間では結婚式の予約を受け付けるまでになりました。

同胞のことは夫だけが頑張っていたのではありません。私も昭和二十七年（一九五二）から民団婦人会に入り、会長を務めてきました。

昭和三十四年ぐらいから、「被爆者手帳を取りませんか？」という話はあったのですが、その頃は、被爆者と分かると仕事などに影響すると言われていたので、夫も「被爆者手帳を貰ったら永久に記録が残るからやめよう」と言いました。

ところが昭和四十六年頃、夫の喉の具合が悪くなったのです。被爆者手帳があると医療費が無料になるというので申請し、「二次被爆患者」と認定されました。

昭和五十八年（一九八三）、夫が「鈍痛がする」というので近くの病院で診てもらいましたが、なかなか良くなりません。

原爆病院に行くと、即、入院することになりました。

「がんが膵臓から肝臓に転移しているので、手のほどこしようがない」と医師に言われましたが、本人には「胃の具合がちょっと悪い程度」としか伝えられませんでした。

だんだん痩せていく夫の顔を見るのが辛く、病院から帰ってきて一人になると、いつも泣いていました。

入院から四カ月ほどで夫は亡くなりました。朝の三時頃でした。「オモニ、カムニダ（おまえ、先に行くよ）」と韓国語で呟くように言って目を閉じたのです。

その後、当時、四歳だった妹の英子（私と十五歳離れている）は血液がん（多発性骨髄腫）に、一歳になったばかりの末の妹・松子も原因不明の足の痛みで手術をしました。

あの日、英子は母に手を引かれ、松子は母に背負われて電車に乗り、駅前のクリーニング店に入る直前に原爆が落ちたのです。戸外での直接被爆でした。

被爆者はみんな、「いつ症状が出るか」と不安をかかえています。私も膝を曲げたりすると痺(しび)れて立てなくなり、「これは原爆のせいかな」と、つい思ってしまいます。

私は、毎年、原爆記念日の平和式典にはチマチョゴリを着て参列します。

「ここに眠る同胞たちの家族はもうほとんどがお参りには来られない。そ

193　　権　舜琴

の人のためにも正装でお参りしてあげたい」という、深い思いがあるからです。

二〇一〇年八月五日、平和式典に来られた潘基文（パン・ギムン）国連事務総長と在日韓国人被爆者として会見しました。

予定にはなかったのですが、原爆資料館の「平和学習室」で三十人ほどの参列者と潘基文事務総長をお迎えしたとき、私のチマチョゴリ姿を見つけられ、すっと近づいてこられ、握手をしてくださいました。「ようこそお越しくださいました」と韓国語でご挨拶（あいさつ）すると、ニコッとされました。

その後、爆心地公園で「核兵器廃絶には一生懸命に取り組む！」と事務総長から言っていただき、大変、印象深く受け止めました。

十七歳で特攻隊員となり、「死」を覚悟していた

馬場 博 さん

ばば・ひろし　一九二五年（大正十四年）十二月生まれ。「飛行機乗り」に憧れ、十七歳のときに志願兵として熊本「陸軍六五部隊」に入隊。後に陸軍飛行学校へ異動になり、特攻隊員となる。出撃日を目前に終戦。爆心地にあった実家では、母と姉一家が亡くなっていた。戦後、三菱造船所で定年まで勤め上げ、結婚して二女に恵まれる。八十九歳。長崎市石神町在住。

出撃三日前に終戦を迎えたが、実家と家族は跡形もなくなっていた

　馬場博さんの家は、山里町（現在の平和町）二三三五番地にあった。爆心地のすぐそばだ。近くには長崎大学のグラウンドがあり、大学生がいつも陸上競技やラグビーの練習をしていた。このグラウンドの脇に大きな楠があって、秋にたくさんの実をつける。この実を竹筒鉄砲の弾丸にするため、馬場さんはよくこの木に登って守衛さんに怒られたという。

　父は私が一歳のときに結核で亡くなり、母は女手ひとつで七歳年上の姉と私を育ててくれました。三十三歳で未亡人になった母は、いち早く布団綿の打ち直し機を購入して、一人で布団綿の打ち直しの仕事を始めました。私が国民学校を卒業した頃、姉はすでに結婚して二人の娘がいました。

昭和十五年（一九四〇）、十四歳で山里国民学校を卒業すると、私は三菱兵器製作所の職工学校に入学し、毎日、戦闘機から魚雷を安定して投下させるための安定器を製造していました。

学校といっても、そこは精密機械工場で他に銃座や針路器などを製造しており、授業は週に二回だけ。ほとんどの時間を、兵器製造に費やしていました。

戦闘機の魚雷安定器を造っていたこともあり、私が憧れていたのは何といっても「飛行機乗り」です。

ところが、予科練の実地試験では、「座った椅子を回転させた後、白線の上を歩かせる」という平衡感覚試験で失敗。私は三菱兵器製作所の職工学校を三年で卒業し、千葉の陸軍戦車学校に行くことになったのです。

陸軍戦車学校は、「学校」となっているが、「戦車による特攻隊養成所」だった。半年後、馬場さんは九州・宮崎の独立戦車隊一二三五部隊に配属となる。

ところが戦況がますます悪化し、沖縄戦では戦闘機乗りが足りなくなったため、馬場さんを含め五人だけが福岡の大刀洗陸軍飛行学校へ異動になった。いきなり、飛行機乗りの訓練を受けることになったのだ。

「即席」の戦闘機乗りの訓練は厳しいものでした。半年間の訓練で沖縄戦に送り込むため、朝から晩まで急発進、急降下の飛行訓練。ほとんど、寝かせてもらえません。

就寝時間に寝床に入っても、「非常講習」といって夜中の一時～二時に抜き打ちの夜間飛行演習があります。その上、何かあるとすぐに往復ビンタが飛んでくるのです。

また、「基礎訓練」では、一晩中、グラウンドを倒れるまで走らされました。私たちのような志願兵は、入隊と同時に「特攻」が義務付けられていたので容赦ありませんでした。
あまりの厳しさに耐えられず、銃剣の先に付ける、通称「ゴボウ剣」で腹を突いて自決した同僚もいたほどです。

こうして半年の訓練を終えて、馬場さんら三人が鹿児島・知覧特攻基地に送られた。知覧行きが決まった日、馬場さんは長崎の母と姉夫婦に遺書を書き、髪と爪を切って同封して送った。
このとき、すでに出撃日は決まっていたが、本人に知らされたのは、前日の夕方だった。
馬場さんは八月九日に知覧特攻基地の三角兵舎に入った。この日は奇しくも長崎に原爆が落とされた日だった。

翌十日のことです。明け方、私は一度小用に起き、それから起床までの間、うつらうつらしながら夢を見ていました。花畑の中に、母と姉夫婦、その二人の娘たちがいて、前に川が流れています。ひとまたぎすれば越えられそうな川を、飛び越えて行こうとする私に「来ちゃダメ！」と、みんなが手を振って止めているのでした。

もしかしたら、母たちは、あの時間に亡くなったのかもしれない、と後になって私は思いました。

特攻隊の三角兵舎は狭く、六、七人も入ればいっぱいの広さでした。そこでは外部との接触を断ち、出撃当日までの日を過ごします。隊員同士が親しくなって、未練が残るような話になってもいけないので、部屋でただゴロゴロ寝ているか、裏山を一人で散歩するぐらいしか、する

ことはありませんでした。死を決めているので、互いに話をすることもありません。他のことは何も考えませんでした。

出撃は未明に行われます。一度に三、四人が出撃するのです。朝、起きたら数人いなくなっていて、すぐに補充の員数が入ってくるので、嫌でも次が自分の番だと分かります。私の出撃予定日は十八日でした。沖縄戦に向かうので、目印は開聞岳です。そこを目指して、飛ぶのです。

八月十五日の昼過ぎ、突然、上官から呼ばれ、「終戦になった。戦争は終わった！」と言われましたが、私は、とっさに意味が理解できませんでした。玉音放送も聞かされなかったのです。

私は、敵艦に体当たりして死ぬ日を待っていただけに、呆然としました。上官の「階級章を外せ！」という怒鳴り声にわれに返り、戦争が終わったことが、ようやく自覚できました。

同時に、いままで張りつめていたものがまたたく間に消えて、腰が抜けたようになってしまいました。
他の隊員たちもうなだれたり、うずくまったりしたまま、焦点の合わない目で、ぼーっとしていました。

「おまえたちは即座に、原隊に戻れ！」と言われ、馬場さんは宮崎の独立戦車隊一二三五部隊に戻った。武装解除になったので、そこで米軍に引き渡すための戦車の整備をしたという。

鹿児島・知覧ではなにごともなかったが、宮崎の原隊では上官にいじめられた若い召集兵が、「もう、上官も二等兵もない！」と、機関銃を撃って暴れていた。

数日後、馬場さんは副官から、「長崎に新型爆弾が落とされたらしい。すぐに長崎に帰れ」と言われた。

この頃になって、やっと、生きている喜びとともに故郷の懐かしさが蘇(よみがえ)ってきました。死ぬことばかり考えていた自分の中に人間らしい感情が戻ってきたのです。

私が職工学校を終えて千葉の戦車隊に入隊するとき、最後に会った母や姉夫婦、その二人の娘、ミッちゃん（光子、四歳）、テルちゃん（輝子、二歳）の顔が思い出されました。

戦車学校は兵隊養成学校なので、三菱の職工学校を終わると一度、形だけ軍隊に所属します。私は熊本の「陸軍六五部隊」に配属になり、そこから戦車学校へ行きました。

「志願兵として熊本に行く」と私が言ったとき、母は寂しそうな顔をして、

「まだ早か！　徴兵検査（十九歳）まで待たんば」と、叫びました。

「母さんや姉さんを守るために行くんや」と、私が言い返すと、母は黙って下を向いてしまいました。

そこで、急遽、姉夫婦が母と同居するために引っ越してきたのです。ミっちゃんとテルちゃんとはそのときに会いました。二人は「ちょうど良い遊び相手」とばかりに、「お兄ちゃん、お兄ちゃん」と言って、私から離れません。

わずか二、三日でしたが、長崎大学のグラウンドや金比羅山の麓にある穴弘法に連れて行ったことも懐かしい思い出です。

浦上駅から出征する私を、母は「愛国婦人会」のたすきを掛け、日の丸の旗を振って見送ってくれました。思えば、上海事変、満州事変、日中戦争と、私はずっと戦争の中で少年時代を過ごしたことになります。

戦争が終わって長崎に帰るにあたり、上官に「義理の兄（姉の夫）は煙

草が好きなので、持って行ってやりたいのですが」と言うと、「いくらでも持って行け」と酒保（軍事施設に設けられた売店のこと）を開けてくれました。
「好きなだけ」と言われたので、五百本まとめて雑囊に入れ、みっちゃんとテルちゃんの土産には、戦車隊にだけ配給されていたチョコレート二十枚と、金平糖入りの甘い乾パンを十袋、雑囊に詰めるだけ詰めました。
「みっちゃん、テルちゃんとは二年半会っていないけど、あの年頃の子は大きくなるのも早いから、かなり大きくなっているだろうな」「会っても、分かるかな」と、思ったりしながら、私は、チョコや乾パンを前に二人が大はしゃぎする様子を想像しました。
また、姉の夫・末五郎さんが煙草をうまそうに吸っている姿を思い浮かべ、どんなに喜んでくれるかと、一人ニヤニヤしてしまうのでした。

宮崎から長崎に着くまで三日間かかった。浦上駅に着いたときの衝撃は、

とても言葉で表せないものだったという。駅舎らしいものは無く、トタン屋根を打ち付けた三角兵舎のようなバラックから、駅員が出てきた。原爆投下から一カ月以上経っているのに死体を片づける人もなく、白骨が散らばっている。腐乱した死体にはウジがたかって部分、部分が白くなっていた。あまりの臭いに圧倒され、馬場さんは歩くこともできなかったという。

　ともかく、私は実家を探しに行きました。山里町は爆心地なので、一面焼け野原で、どこがどこだか分からないほどでした。私は、よく遊びに行った小さな森を見つけ、そこから通学路とおぼしきところをたどり、うろうろしていると、見覚えのある井戸と焼け残った布団綿打ち直し機の鉄骨を発見したのです。
　わが家の跡を確認し、唖然(あぜん)としました。

馬場　博

母は、姉夫婦は、ミっちゃんやテルちゃんはどこへ行ったんだ？　わが家の跡を見るまで、母たちは生きているものと思い込んでいただけに、言い知れぬ失望感でいっぱいになりました。

私は仏間の辺りの焦土を、母の遺骨代わりにと飯盒に詰めました。橋の下で寝ようと思ったのですが、川には牛や馬、人間の死体がいっぱい浮いているのです。同じ死体のそばで寝るなら墓場がいいだろうと、私はわが家の墓地に行って寝ました。

ともかく、「食うためには、働かなくては」と思い、翌日、三菱兵器製作所に顔を出すと、三菱の職工学校卒業ということで、すぐに雇ってくれました。

けれど、そのときの仕事は、長崎の四大三菱（造船、製鋼、電機、製作所）工場に放置されていた遺体の収容だったのです。長崎に残っている男た

は、怪我人と火傷を負った人しかおらず、元気なのは兵隊帰りだけだったからです。

腐ってドロドロの遺体の衣服から名前を探し出し、「名前のある遺体」と「無い遺体」に分けて焼きました。

私は三菱造船所に、そのまま定年まで勤めました。二十三歳の時、母の弟の紹介で長崎・大村の女性と結婚。二人の娘にも恵まれました。昭和二十九年（一九五四）、長崎・大村に両親の墓を建てました。父の遺骨の中に、母の遺骨代わりの焦土を入れ、一つにして。これが、私ができる唯一の親孝行でした。

馬場　博

［被爆証言を読んで①］

不戦の誓いを新たに

長崎大学理事・副学長／福島県立医科大学副学長 山下俊一

原爆被災から七十周年の節目に、創価学会長崎平和委員会が「語りつぐナガサキ」を日英二カ国語で出版される意義と、その歴史的な価値は非常に大きなものがあります。

一長崎市民として、そして一地球市民として心から感謝とお礼を申し上げます。浅学非才の身でありながら、本証言集を読ませていただき感想を

述べさせていただくことは誠に僭越ではありますが、原爆医療そして世界の放射線災害医療に携わる医師として、過去の教訓を真摯に学び将来の糧にさせていただく所存です。核戦争に対して医学や医療は無力であればこそ、核兵器の使用は決して許してはならず、広島と長崎の原爆証言集が、核兵器廃絶と恒久平和を希求する根幹となります。

 二〇一四年、すでに創価学会広島平和委員会が「男たちのヒロシマ」を編集されていますが、長い間の沈黙を破った十四人の貴重な広島の証言が生々しく取り上げられ、読む人すべてに深い悲しみと言葉に言い表せない強い憤りを感じさせます。人類史上初めて広島、そして長崎の両市民が無差別核攻撃に曝されたことは、戦争悪の極限を垣間みる思いであり、人類史の最大の汚点です。

 今回の長崎からの証言集二〇一五年では、新たに被爆女性の視点が加わり、戦争の悲惨さと放射線被曝の深刻さのみならず、何よりも生まれてく

る子どもたちへの不安と恐怖がどれだけ母親を苦しめ続けたかを思い知らされました。まさに沈黙の中で精神心理的、そして社会的な苦痛を長きにわたり抱え込まざるを得ないという理不尽な仕打ちが明白であります。十四人全員の長崎原爆被災後の過酷な人生の歩みに思いを馳（は）せるときに、まさに歴史を学ぶとは、過去に囚（とら）われることではなく、未来に責任を持ち一人一人が不戦の誓いを新たにすることだと言えます。

記録された一つ一つの貴重な証言には、それを咀嚼（そしゃく）し理解し、次に繋（つな）げる責務と覚悟を促す強いメッセージが含まれています。原爆被災を決して過去のこと、そして他人事としてではなく、自分事として、他者の痛みを共有することが重要となります。何事も風評被害や風化現象は避けられませんが、過ちが繰り返される危険があるからこそ、如何（いか）なる場合においても謙虚に、そして正しく証言集を語り継ぐ努力が求められます。混乱と混迷、そして矛盾の多い現代社会であればこそ、一人一人が心の安寧を保ち、

平和希求の精神を基本として、普段の日常生活においても不正に身を委ねることなく、言葉の暴力を避け、異なる価値観を積み重ねる努力が必要です。無知、無関心に配慮したコミュニケーションを積み重ねる努力が必要です。無知、無関心、そして誤解や偏見、先入観を乗り越えるためにも広島、長崎の原爆被災の実相を正しく伝えたいと存じます。

最後に、原爆被災で無念のうちに亡くなられたすべての犠牲者のご冥福をお祈り申し上げるとともに、長きにわたり原爆の身体的な後遺症と心の傷を背負い続けておられる被爆者の平穏な毎日を心から祈念申し上げます。

[被爆証言を読んで②]

十四人の苦難の自分史

長崎原爆病院名誉院長／核廃絶地球市民集会ナガサキ実行委員長

朝長万左男

十四人のヒバクシャの七十年の自分史を読み、あらためて原爆がヒバクシャの人生を翻弄(ほんろう)し続けた現実に衝撃を受けると同時に、深い感動を覚えます。家族を亡くし、自らの健康を損ない、財産を失い、経済的にも恵まれなかった七十年の人生は、十四人の方々それぞれに多様ですが、原爆によって狂わされたという一点だけは共通であり、これは広島・長崎の全ヒ

バクシャにおいて、そうであろうと肯(うなず)かされます。原爆の悲惨さはまさにこの全人的影響にあることにあらためて気付かされます。

なかでも、いつかは原爆の後遺症が出るのではないかという不安、やっとの思いで結婚したものの、生まれてくるわが子に放射線による遺伝の影響はないかと恐れる心情は、想像を絶するものがあります。結婚に際しては、被爆しなかった人々からの差別的な言動に一様に苦しんだことが胸に刺さります。

とくに女性の方々の妊娠出産時の苦悩はいかばかりであったでしょう。皆さんがそのような苦難の人生を生き抜いて、七十年の節目に自分史を克明に、しかも淡々と書かれています。絶望の中から強靱(きょうじん)な意志で立ち上がり、家族を持ち、苦難の人生に活路を見いだし、いまの自分があることを謙虚に綴(つづ)っておられ、まさに全人的強さがひしひしと伝わってきます。繰り返し過ごされた夏が二〇一五年またやってきます。

このように、ヒロシマ・ナガサキの二十万人を超えるヒバクシャが生き抜いた二十万の七十年が原爆であったと言えるでしょう。

一九四五年七月の人類史上初めての核爆発実験が米国アラモゴードで成功して以来七十年の歳月が流れました。未来の人類史には、一九四五年から始まり、ついに核兵器保有と原子力利用が終焉を迎える年（願わくば）で終わるまでの時代を、「核時代 Nuclear Age」と表記することになることは間違いないでしょう。

人類が古代から築いてきた文明の背後には、連綿と続く武器の発達と戦争の高度化がありました。その歴史において、人類が初めて直面した「自らの絶滅」を可能とする核兵器の登場は、核時代の幕開け初頭に、二十万人の死者とそれを超えるヒバクシャを生み出しました。その後も核実験によるヒバクシャ、原発事故の被害者と続く「核の被害者」の群れが存在し

続けることが、この核時代の最大の特徴であり、これらの人々こそ核時代そのものの体現者であり、証人であると言えます。人類が二十一世紀にも繁栄を続けていくとすれば、これらの人々は繁栄の犠牲者と呼べるでしょう。

通常の戦災、すなわち戦略爆撃と呼ばれる東京大空襲や沖縄戦のような戦闘での被害と原爆の被害の最も歴然とした違いは、原爆では放射線による健康障害が生涯続くという点にあるでしょう。がんなどの健康障害が実際にわが身に起こってくる恐怖は、まだ発病していない健康なときも、ヒバクシャの心を常にむしばんできたことが十四人の自分史からも切々と伝わってきます。その恐怖心をよく耐え忍んで、心配した遺伝的な影響も乗り越えることができた人生がある一方、不運にも心配が現実のものとなった人生もあって、それらを乗り越えてきたことに、人としての強靭さを感じさせられます。

217　被爆証言を読んで②　朝長万左男

われわれ被爆医療の専門家は、そのような被爆者の健康障害を、被爆距離や被曝線量から調べて分析し、近距離かつ被曝線量の高い人ほど強く健康障害が現れたことを明らかにしてきました。リスクの高いことを数字から読み取ることは簡単にできても、ここに書かれたヒバクシャの原爆から受けた影響の全体像については、ほんの一部しか窺い知ることができないことも痛感します。二十万人のヒバクシャが生きた人生は、距離や線量では計測できない、等しく苦難の人生であり、並外れた強靱さを強いられたものであったのです。

放射線による健康障害は、被爆距離と線量という不平等の中から生じてきましたが、ヒバクシャの人生は等しく原爆の影響下にあったのです。国のヒバクシャに対するさまざまな支援もずいぶん良くなったとはいえ、いまだに健康障害に苦しむ人々、適切な経済支援の受けられない人々、遺伝的影響を心配し続ける人々を生み出し続けています。いまや平均年齢は七

十八歳を超え、子どものときに被爆した方々がほとんどという状況になっています。

一九四五年八月に瞬間的に被爆したことで、七十年の生涯にわたって持続するこの諸々の影響を免れ得ないことが、まさに核兵器の本質と言わざるを得ません。国の政策にもこのことの理解がまったく足りません。放射線の被曝量とその影響の現れた証拠のみを根拠とする国の政策においては、この核時代の本質が見落とされているといわざるを得ません。十四人の方々の自分史がまさにこのことを証明しているといってよいでしょう。

最後に、人類が核の廃絶についに成功し、人間としての叡智をもつことが証明されることを願って、十四人のヒバクシャの自分史執筆に感謝の誠を捧げます。

219　被爆証言を読んで②　朝長万左男

We specialists in medical care for radiation exposure have analyzed the physical disorders of survivors in terms of distance and dose. We have shown beyond doubt that the closer to the bomb and the higher the dose, the greater the physical harm. Our figures reveal high risks and physical harm easily, but the full effects of the atomic bombing can never be quantified. Our figures reveal only a tiny fraction of the damage done. The suffering inflicted in hundreds of thousands of disrupted lives can never be correlated to distance or dose. The lives of most hibakusha have been extremely difficult, and many still are, all because of the bomb.

The physical disorders due to radiation derive from unequal distances and doses, but, in a way, the bombing influenced all hibakusha equally. Although assistance from the national government has improved, many hibakusha are still suffering from illness, lack of sufficient financial assistance, and anxiety over genetic effects. The average age of the hibakusha is now over 78; most of them were exposed when they were quite young. Thus, an instantaneous exposure in August 1945 has kept survivors imprisoned by aftereffects for 70 years. This imprisonment is in the nature of nuclear weapons. The national government's measures are inadequate. To the extent that the government bases its assistance on dose and proven effects, I say it ignores the essence of the nuclear age. The 14 eyewitness accounts in this book testify to this reality.

I close with the hope that humankind will demonstrate its wisdom by abolishing nuclear weapons, and with my profound gratitude to the 14 hibakusha for sharing their stories.

arose from the depths of despair with nothing but an indomitable will. They built families, found ways to surmount obstacles, and stand before us describing those lives and feelings openly and humbly. In these stories, we cannot help but perceive enormous strength and humanity.

Seventy years have passed since July 1945 when the US successfully conducted its Trinity Test in the desert near Alamogordo, New Mexico. I have no doubt that 1945 to the end of nuclear weapons will be called the Nuclear Age, a dark and dangerous period of human history. Behind the many human civilizations that have risen and fallen since ancient times we have seen the consistent development of weapons and concomitant intensification of war. The nuclear age started off by killing over 200,000 people, leaving hundreds of thousands of suffering hibakusha. It went on to give our species the power to extinguish itself. Throughout, the Nuclear Age has generated group after group of hibakusha, the victims of nuclear tests and accidents. These hibakusha are eyewitnesses but also embodiments of the distinguishing characteristic of the Nuclear Age. If human beings continue to prosper in 21st century, these hibakusha should be numbered among the victims of that prosperity.

The Great Tokyo Air Raid, the Battle of Okinawa, and firebombing with conventional weapons did tremendous damage, but the most obvious difference between these acts of war and the atomic bombings is the never-ending threat and harm to health from radiation. The fear of contracting cancer tortures survivors even when they are healthy, a reality we see clearly in the stories of the 14 witnesses in this book. Some withstood those fears and were spared the effects, while others, unfortunately, saw their fears come true. But all overcame great suffering and demonstrated the unyielding power of human dignity.

Reading Eyewitness Testimonies 2
Stories of Suffering from 14 Survivors

Masao Tomonaga
Director Emeritus, Nagasaki Atomic Bomb Hospital
Chairman of the Organizing Committee
Nagasaki Global Citizens' Assembly for the Elimination of Nuclear Weapons

After reading the 14 stories in this book, I am shocked once again by the extent to which the atomic bombing affected every aspect of survivors' lives. In the course of 70 years, they have lost family members, suffered health effects, lost property and struggled economically. The stories vary, but they have in common the obvious fact that their whole lives were horribly damaged and disrupted by the atomic bombing. The same must be true of nearly all the survivors of Hiroshima and Nagasaki, reminding me once again that an atomic bombing harms the entirety of the human beings involved.

The anxiety survivors still feel regarding potential aftereffects emerging in their own bodies or genetic effects emerging in their offspring is quite beyond imagination for those of us who don't have it. And because of that anxiety in others, they were discriminated against even in marriage. The pain they experienced due to words and rejection by the unexposed pierces my heart.

Think how horribly the women suffered when pregnant and delivering babies! So many have lived such difficult lives, but they handled their ordeals philosophically with a profound grace. Many

by the atomic bombings. I also pray for the happiness of the survivors, many of whom still suffer, after 70 years, from the physical and psychological wounds inflicted by the atomic bombings.

indiscriminate nuclear attacks offers a glimpse into the extreme evil of war. These bombings will always stand out as ugly stains on human history.

This Telling the Story of Nagasaki offers a number of accounts from a woman's viewpoint. The atrocity of war and horror of radiation are conveyed, but we look as well into the fear of childbirth, a fear that tortured so many exposed mothers. These stories help us see that mothers were unfairly and cruelly forced to endure terrible psychological and social pain, and to bear it all in silence over years and even decades. When we contemplate the harsh lives the 14 survivors suffered after the atomic bombing, we are reminded that to learn history is not loitering in the past; it is taking responsibility for the future. In this context, each of us must renew our absolute renunciation of war.

Every one of these valuable testimonies contains a strong message urging us to appreciate and understand what happened and recognize our responsibility to the next generation. We must not study the atomic bombings as history or tragedies that happened to someone else. We must share the pain, accepting it as our own. We are often unable to avoid the problems of rumor and fading memory. Because of the danger that the error will be repeated, we must make every effort to pass on survivor testimonies humbly and correctly. Contemporary society is filled with confusion, turmoil and contradiction. Therefore, each of us must keep our own minds peaceful and maintain the peace-seeking spirit. We need to communicate our caring for others without excluding those who are different. We must avoid violence, even violent words, by rooting out wrongdoing in daily life. I seek to convey the facts of Hiroshima and Nagasaki correctly to overcome ignorance, indifference, misunderstanding, prejudice and preconceived ideas.

In closing, I pray for the repose of the precious souls taken from us

Reading Eyewitness Testimonies 1
Renewing the Renunciation of War

Shun-ichi Yamashita

Vice President / Trustee, Nagasaki University
Vice President, Fukushima Medical University

The fact that the Soka Gakkai Nagasaki Peace Committee is commemorating the 70th anniversary of the atomic bombing of Nagasaki by publishing *Nagasaki August 9, 1945* in both Japanese and English carries profound significance and social value. As a citizen of Nagasaki and a member of the global community, I would like to express my sincere gratitude and appreciation.

I have been asked to offer my impression of the book, but I feel incapable of doing it justice. As a physician engaged in medical care related to the A-bomb and radiation, I am continually learning lessons from the past and using them to guide my future. Because medical science and medical care are helpless against a nuclear attack, we must never allow another use of a nuclear weapon. Thus, we must use the atomic bomb survivor stories from Hiroshima and Nagasaki as our guides to genuine and lasting peace in a nuclear-weapon-free world.

In 2014 the Soka Gakkai Hiroshima Peace Committee compiled Hiroshima August 6, 1945. The precious testimonies of 14 Hiroshima survivors, all of whom broke long silences to describe their experiences, help readers peer into deep sorrow and inexpressible rage. That the citizens of both Hiroshima and Nagasaki were the targets of

me.

Searching for nametags or other identification, I examined the clothes of the rotten, melting corpses, classifying them as "corpses with names" and "corpses without names." Then, I incinerated them.

I worked for the Mitsubishi Shipyard until retirement. I married a woman from Omura, Nagasaki Prefecture introduced to me by my mother's younger brother when I was 23. We were blessed with two daughters.

I built my parents' grave in Omura in 1954. I mixed the earth I was keeping as my mother's remains in with my father's ashes. This was the best I could do to show my devotion to my parents.

He felt too weak to walk.

I went looking for my house, of course. Since Yamazato-machi was close to the hypocenter, the whole area was a burnt plain. It had all disappeared to such an extent I couldn't tell where I was. I found a grove of trees I had often played in and followed the road that looked like the one I had used to get to school. I kept looking around and eventually found a well I knew. I also found the iron skeleton of a burnt futon reconditioning machine. In utter amazement, I realized that I was looking at the ruins of my house.

Where was my mother? Where were my sister and her husband? Where were Mitsuko and Teruko? I had assumed that I would find my family alive until I saw what had become of my house. I cannot express the horror and grief that spread through my heart.

Because I couldn't find any trace of my mother, I collected burnt earth near the spot I thought our Buddhist altar had been. I put the earth in my water bottle and took it with me as her remains.

I thought I would sleep under a bridge but there were too many dead cows, horses and human bodies floating on the river. If I had to sleep beside dead bodies, I would sleep in a graveyard. I went to my family's graveyard and slept there.

The first thing I thought was, "In order to eat, I have to work." The next day I showed up at Mitsubishi Ordnance Works. When I told them I had graduated from their Craftsman's School, they hired me immediately. However, the job they gave me was to dispose of the human remains abandoned in Nagasaki's Big Four Mitsubishi Factories (the shipyard, steel works, electric and ordnance works). Almost all the men in Nagasaki were burned or injured in some way. Those healthy enough to work were all ex-soldiers coming home, like

Nagasaki August 9, 1945

My mother saw me off at Urakami Station wearing the Women's Patriotic Association sash and waving a Japanese flag. Thinking back on my life, I see that my entire boyhood was spent in wartime, from the Shanghai Incident to the Manchurian Incident and the Sino-Japanese War.

Now, the war had ended, and I was going back to Nagasaki. Speaking to my senior officer, I said, "My brother-in-law likes cigarettes, and I want to take him some." He said, "Take as many as you like," and he opened the commissary.

Because he said "as many as you like," I took about 500 cigarettes and put them in my pack. For Mitsuko and Teruko, I grabbed 20 chocolate bars that had been supplies for the tank unit and 10 bags of sweet dry bread with crunchy sugar balls in it. I packed as much as I could into my pack. Thinking, "I haven't seen Mitsuko and Teruko for two and a half years. Girls at that age grow up fast, so they must be little ladies by now." I wondered if I would be able to recognize them. I imagined how excited they would be seeing the chocolate and sweet bread.

I also had an image of my sister's husband's face smoking the cigarettes. I grinned just thinking how happy he would be.

It took three days for Hiroshi to reach Nagasaki from Miyazaki. Arriving at Urakami Station, his shock was indescribable. There was no station building. The station staff came out of a shabby shack with a galvanized tin sheet roof.

More than a month had passed since the atomic bombing, but nobody was disposing of the corpses and white skeletons scattered all around. Maggots swarmed in decomposing bodies, appearing as white spots. Hiroshi was overwhelmed by the stench.

No trouble occurred at Chiran Base, but in his original unit in Miyazaki a young drafted soldier who had been teased brutally by his superior officers became violent, spraying bullets from a machine gun shouting, "No more officers, no more privates!"

A few days later, an Adjutant told Hiroshi that a new type of bomb was dropped on Nagasaki. "Go home now."

By that time, the joy of being alive as well as fond memories of my hometown had revived me at last. Human feelings welled up in me. From being a young man thinking of nothing but death, I was suddenly recalling the faces of my mother, my sister, her husband, and their daughters Mitsuko (4) and Teruko (2). I had last seen them when I finished Craftsman's School and enrolled in the tank school in Chiba.

That tank school had been soldier training, so, as a matter of form, I had to belong to a military unit. I was assigned to "Army Unit 65" in Kumamoto and went to tank school from there.

"I'm going to Kumamoto as a volunteer soldier." When I told my mother, she looked so sad and shouted, "It's too early! Please wait two more years and pass your enlistment examination."

I answered, "I'm going to protect you and my sister." She became silent and looked down. Because I was leaving, my sister's family hurriedly moved into my house to live with my mother. That's when I met Mitsuko and Teruko. The two girls seemed to regard me as the perfect playmate. They never left me alone, hanging around me like little sisters.

I was with them only a few days, but taking them to Nagasaki University Sports Field and Ana Kobo Temple at the foot of Mt. Konpira are good memories for me.

spent the time alone, and there was not much to do. I stayed in my room lying down or hiking up the hill behind the building. Because I was ready to die, I had nothing to say to anyone. I had nothing but my death to think about.

We sent a sortie out before daybreak. Three or four pilots took off at the same time. I woke up one morning and found that a few comrades had gone and replacements would be arriving soon. By then it was obvious that I would be the next to go. I was scheduled to leave on the 18th.

Because my landmark was Kaimondake, a cone-shaped volcano on the southern tip of the Satsuma Peninsula in Kagoshima, I would be flying straight toward the volcano to fly to Okinawa.

My superior officer called me in the afternoon of August 15th to say, "The war ended. The war is over!" He said it, but I couldn't take it in. It took a while to understand and accept. We had not been allowed to hear the broadcast in which the Emperor announced Japan's surrender, and because I had been waiting to die by flying into an enemy warship, the call just left me dazed.

I came back to myself when my superior officer yelled, "Take your badge off!" At that instant, I finally realized that the war was over.

At the same time my strained nerves, which I had kept under such strict control for so long, suddenly failed me. I could hardly keep standing. Some stood with heads hung low. Others squatted down, their eyes staring vacantly at nothing.

The suddenly freed kamikaze were told to "…return to your original units immediately!" Hiroshi went back to Tank Unit 1235 in Miyazaki. Disarmament had begun, so he repaired or maintained tanks to be handed over to the US army.

was called "emergency training." If I failed to do the exercise, I got a double slap on my face. Then, I was forced to run around the field all night until I collapsed. This was "basic training." Volunteers like me were destined to fly a "suicide attack" as soon as we enlisted, so we received no mercy. One comrade stabbed his own stomach because he couldn't bear the harshness.

After six months of this severe training, Hiroshi and two other comrades were sent to Chiran Kamikaze Base in Kagoshima. The day he was sent to Chiran he wrote a will to his mother, his sister and her husband in Nagasaki. He cut his nails and a lock of hair and sent those along with his will. By that time his flight was already scheduled, but he was not informed until the evening before he was supposed to fly. He moved to the barracks at the Chiran Base on August 9th, the day the atomic bomb destroyed Nagasaki.

The following day, the 10th, I woke up at dawn to go to the bathroom. I came back to my bed half asleep and had a dream that lasted until reveille. My mother, my sister, her husband and their two daughters were in a field of flowers with a stream running between us. The stream was small enough to get over in a single bound. I was just about to jump across when they stopped me. They were waving their hands saying, "Don't come over here!" Later, I learned that they had all died in the bombing.

The Kamikaze Corps barracks were small. Six or seven of us made them quite full. We lost contact with the outside world and spent our days waiting to fly.

To avoid making friends and getting attached to each other, we

Nagasaki August 9, 1945

I graduated from Yamazato Elementary School in 1940 at 14. I entered the Craftsman's School at Mitsubishi Ordnance Works and worked every day manufacturing the stabilizers designed to drop well-balanced torpedoes from fighter planes.

We called it a school but it was a precision machine shop that manufactured gun emplacements, course indicators, and other similar devices. We had lessons only twice a week and spent most of the time making weapons.

I was making torpedo stabilizers for fighter planes, but what I really wanted to do was fly the planes. I took a field test offered by the naval preparatory course for student aviators. I failed the balance test, which involved sitting on a chair as it spun around, then walking a straight white line. I graduated from Craftsman's School in three years and was assigned to the Army Tank School in Chiba.

The Army Tank School was also called a "school," but it was actually a kamikaze training facility that used tanks. Half a year later, Hiroshi was assigned to Independent Tank Unit 1235 in Miyazaki, Kyushu. However, the war was going badly for Japan, and fighter pilots were in short supply. Thus, five soldiers, including Hiroshi, were sent to the Tachiarai Army Aviation Academy in Fukuoka to prepare for the Battle of Okinawa. All of a sudden, Hiroshi was being trained to fly an airplane after all.

The training for "instant fighter pilots" was merciless. To send us to Okinawa with a half-year of training, we were trained in quick takeoffs and nosedives from morning till night. We hardly spent any time in bed. Even after going to bed, we could be called without previous notice to "night flight exercises" at one or two in the morning. This

Joining the Kamikaze when I was 17, I was prepared for death.

Hiroshi Baba
Born December 1925. Dreaming of being an airplane pilot, joined Army Unit 65 in Kumamoto as a volunteer when he was 17. Later transferred to Army Aviation Academy, assigned to the Kamikaze Corps. Just before he was scheduled to fly his suicide mission, the war ended. In his house near the hypocenter, his mother and his sister's entire family were killed. After the war, worked for Mitsubishi Shipyard until retirement. Married, was blessed with two daughters. Eighty-nine years old; resides in Ishigami-machi, Nagasaki City.

The war ended three days before my mission.
My house and family were gone without a trace.

Hiroshi Baba's house was at 235 Yamazato-machi (now, Heiwa-machi), very close to the hypocenter. In a sports field near his house belonging to Nagasaki University, students were routinely practicing track and field or rugby. A big camphor tree near this field produced thousands of nuts every fall. Hiroshi often climbed that tree to gather nuts to use as bullets in his bamboo tube gun. He was scolded by a security guard.

My father died of tuberculosis when I was one. My mother raised my sister (seven years older) and me all by herself. My mother, a widow at 33, bought one of the first futon reconditioning machines. She began reconditioning futon, doing all the work herself. By the time I graduated from elementary school, my sister was already married and had two daughters.

bombing?"

Every year on August 9, the day of the Nagasaki Peace Ceremony, I attend the ceremony wearing the traditional ch'ima chogori. I have a deep feeling of solidarity with my fellow Koreans who rest here and cannot come to the ceremony. I pray for all of them, and I want to pray for them in my national costume.

On August 5th 2010, as a Korean atomic bomb survivor living in Japan, I met United Nations Secretary-General Ban Ki-moon, who came to attend the Peace Ceremony. That meeting was not in his original schedule, but about 30 of us who attended the ceremony greeted him in the peace study room in the Atomic Bomb Museum. When he saw me in my ch'ima chogori, he quickly came over and shook my hand.

"Welcome to Nagasaki," I said in Korean, and he smiled at me. Later, speaking in the hypocenter park, the Secretary-General told us he would do his best to abolish nuclear weapons. His words made a deep impression on me.

book, it will be on our record forever. Let's not do it."

However, my husband developed a problem in his throat in 1971. We heard that if he had a Survivor Health Book he could get medical treatment for free. We applied for the Health Book and he was identified as a "Residual Radiation-Exposed Patient."

In 1983, my husband said, "I have a dull pain that doesn't go away." We visited a clinic nearby, but his condition did not get better. We visited the Atomic Bomb Hospital and he was immediately admitted. The doctor said, "His cancer has metastasized from the pancreas to the liver. There is nothing we can do." I couldn't tell my husband. I just said, "There seems to be a problem in your stomach."

It was painful to watch my husband's face get thinner and thinner. Whenever I came home from the hospital and was alone, I cried. About four months after entering the hospital, he passed away. It was around three in the morning. "My love, I'll go on ahead of you." He said this barely audibly in Korean and closed his eyes.

After he died, my sister Hideko, who was 15 years younger than I and four years old at the time of the bombing, contracted multiple myeloma. My youngest sister Matsuko, who was one at the time, underwent surgery for leg pain of unknown cause.

On the day of the bombing, our mother got off a streetcar pulling Hideko by the hand and carrying Matsuko on her back. Just before going into a laundry in front of Nagasaki Station, the atomic bomb exploded. They were exposed outside and directly but at a distance of about 2.3 kilometers from the hypocenter.

Almost all the survivors have a deep anxiety. "When will I develop some disorder?" Personally, my knees get numb when I sit on them and I can't stand up. I can't help thinking, "Is this due to the atomic

in Nagasaki. That was not enough to feed us, so we brewed and sold illegal Korean liquor. However, we were discovered and policemen came to our house. My husband escaped to Osaka but I was left behind. I was arrested and subjected to merciless interrogation. I never wavered in claiming ignorance and denied any involvement. At last the policeman questioning me was so impressed he said, "You are really tough!"

Sun Gun's husband later returned, and the couple started a scrap iron business that involved collecting scrap in a cart and selling it to a trader in Sasebo. In 1963 after saving enough money, they opened a small Korean restaurant called Arirang House. At that time Korean bulgogi was virtually unknown in Japan.

My husband resigned as local chief of the Korean Residents Union in Japan to become chairman of the Nagasaki Commercial Credit Union. He said, "I can't be of any help at the restaurant, so you run it as you like!" I worked hard by myself, and it paid off. We were able to expand the restaurant, eventually becoming a three-story barbecue building. We were so successful we were able to do wedding receptions in our big hall on the 3rd floor.

My husband was not the only one devoted to the Korean community. I joined the Korean Residents Union in Japan Women's Group in 1952 and am still on the advisory board.

Since about 1959 I have often been asked, "Why don't you obtain an Atomic Bomb Survivor Health Book?" I had heard that being a survivor would have a bad influence on a business like ours, so I was reluctant to get the book. My husband also said, "If we get the health

machi, right near the hypocenter. All the camps were gone without a trace. He found no laborers. He didn't know if they were burned to death, buried under debris or had run away. Of his 30 laborers, only two were ever found. Both were dead and were identified on a municipal boat going from Ohato to a worksite.

Daily, my husband made the rounds to all the construction camps looking for our laborers. The only ones he ever found out about were the two on the boat.

It was said that 70,000 Koreans were in the Nagasaki area at that time. Of that number, 20,000 were exposed to the atomic bombing, and 10,000 were killed. I am sure that many of those laborers had been forced to come to Japan.

The situation of my fellow Koreans after the bombing was tragic. Most who survived the bombing had no place to go. Many came to our house begging for something to eat.

Many Koreans with no place to go, including forced laborers, stole radishes from farms or were given potatoes, which they sold near Harusame Bridge. They built shacks in that area, which quickly became a Korean settlement. Maybe because so many Japanese men were away at war, I noticed a number of Japanese women falling in love with Koreans and living with them near the bridge.

Our family had a very hard time, too. My husband received work from the Construction Cooperative Union and worked without his laborers to clean up the ruins of the atomic bombing. My parents went back to South Korea after the war, in October.

We couldn't run construction camps any more, so my husband and I purchased sports shoes from a wholesaler in Kobe and sold them

Nagasaki August 9, 1945

hanging on both ends of a shoulder pole. I did this over and over. It was extremely hard work for my 15-year-old body.

At 18 I married a man who was doing office work under my father. His name was Tho Yon Sik, and he was 11 years older than me. We made a new home on Koyagi Island. Later my husband said, quite seriously, "You are short. I bet that's because you carried all that water when you were still growing."

My husband later quit my father's company and became independent. One reason is because my father enjoyed alcoholic drinks after work but my husband never touched a drop of alcohol. My husband built a new camp in Kosedo, taking in nine laborers.

Around that time, Allied air raids were intensifying. Houses throughout the city required repair, so Sun Gun's husband got plenty of work. He soon had several construction camps housing over 30 laborers. They had no children, so Sun Gun took care of the laborers, going around to the camps with her husband.

On August 9, I went to the Inasa Bridge camp in Asahi-machi to prepare lunch. My husband came in, and just as I was serving him tea, we heard a tremendous booooom. I went outside and saw black smoke rapidly spreading across the sky. Then, it turned pitch black. When the darkness lifted, crowds of badly burnt people were walking single file in front of the bunkhouse. Fires broke out everywhere. I saw horses, cows and numerous dead human bodies floating in the Urakami River.

With no means of transportation, Sun Gun and her husband walked over the mountain and back to Kosedo. The next day her husband visited his construction camps, including the one in Matsuyama-

to bring me an umbrella. I avoided her and went home alone. I was afraid of being insulted even more by my classmates. I apologized to her when I got home. I will never forget my mother's sad face as she said, "These are the only clothes I have."

We moved to Sasebo, Nagasaki Prefecture when I was 15, the year my sister was born. I went to Ainoura Post-Elementary School in Sasebo. My mother was in poor physical condition and said, "Please go to school with your sister on your back." When my sister cried during a lesson, I left the classroom and tried to pacify her in the corridor. Other children walking by us said, "Yarashika, yarashika." I didn't understand Japanese well and thought they were making fun of us. Later, I learned they were saying, "She's cute," in Nagasaki dialect.

My father went back to Korea and recruited laborers for construction work in Japan. He opened a construction camp in Nagasaki. Five or six day laborers at a time would stay in our bunkhouse with its galvanized tin sheet roof.

To tell the truth, I wanted to continue my studies and become a nurse, but my parents wanted me to quit school to help them prepare meals for those laborers.

My father's work camps were mainly on Koyagi Island. Honson was the main community on Koyagi Island, and many Korean forced laborers worked there. They were forced to work night and day on intensive construction rush jobs. I worked with them.

Koyagi Island was a tough worksite for me. There was no water on the island, so we had to bring it in from Nagasaki by boat. One of my tasks as a cook was to carry water from the boat in two big buckets

Nagasaki August 9, 1945

Praying for fellow Koreans killed by the atomic bombing, I attend the Peace Ceremony wearing the traditional ch'ima chogori.

Kwon Sun Gun

Born January 1926 in Andong City, South Korea. Exposed to the atomic bombing in Asahi-machi, 1.8 kilometers from the hypocenter. Later managed construction camps, scrap iron sales, and a Korean barbecue restaurant with her husband. The restaurant was successful and expanded to become a three-story barbecue building. Now, advisory board member for the Korean Residents Union in Japan Women's Group, Nagasaki Chapter. Her late husband was the local chief of the Korean Residents Union in Japan and chairman of Nagasaki Commercial Credit Union. Eighty-nine years old, resides in Doza-machi, Nagasaki City.

After sharing our hard life, suffering from cancer, my husband said, in Korean, "My love, I'll go on ahead."

My mother and I arrived in Kyoto when I was four. My father had come to Japan ahead of us. When he was young, my father was a bit irresponsible. He casually went wherever he wanted to go. Every time he moved, my mother and I chased after him. We moved from place to place in Japan, too, from Yokkaichi to Gifu, Nagoya and Sasebo.

I was in Kyoto until the 4th grade. We were so poor we couldn't buy rice. Because my mother couldn't make rice balls, I was unable to go on school trips. In school I was insulted. "You smell like garlic!" "Stupid Korean!"

My mother came to school on a rainy day wearing a ch'ima chogori

now.

My brother, who looked like a hedgehog because of all the glass piercing his back, still often says, "Something is back there again! Something is hurting me." He goes to the hospital and has the area cut open. A piece of glass is found, and when they remove it, a wart-like scar forms. My brother's back is covered with such warts.

The atomic bombing left scars in mind and body that never disappear.

it rose up to the thickness of fingers. It even looked like fingers spread and reaching out from the opening. When his body got warm at night, the scar got so itchy he could hardly stand it. Each child took turns rubbing his back all night.

Neighbors who lived near the house beneath Sumiyoshi Shrine visited us in Shimabara. They asked us to sell them the beams and pillars of our house, which was collapsed and unlivable. Soon after we gave our consent, the house vanished with no trace of its original form.

That fall those neighbors near Sumiyoshi Shrine visited us again. This time, they said our rice field had produced a fine crop, and they wanted to buy our rice.

We went to the field and found the seedlings my parents had planted in spring ripening abundantly despite complete neglect. We harvested 13 large bags of rice.

In March the following year I took an examination at Girls' Commercial School and graduated. I went to school to get the diploma. There, for the first time, I found out that many of my classmates had died.

After coming back from Shimabara, four of us children (my oldest brother, my third oldest sister, my third oldest brother, who had come back from military service, and myself) reopened the Inoue Laundry near Spectacles Bridge.

At 18, I married a man who was in the same business. My eldest brother introduced him to me. Two years later, we opened our own laundry in Heiwa-machi. We were blessed with six children.

My father's burns healed but he died on January 1, 1951 due to tuberculosis. I had extreme anemia. I used to faint often, but it's better

Teruko's mother's friend's husband, Mr. Kondo, was working for Mitsubishi Ordnance Works. When he rushed home immediately after the bombing he found his youngest daughter (5) trapped under the collapsed house. He was unable to pull his daughter out of the rubble despite best efforts. While trying to get her out, he asked, "Who was here?" She replied, "Brother, Sister and me. And Mommy and Mrs. Inoue (Teruko's mother)." Thus, Teruko heard later that her mother was killed in the Kondos' house.

Because I didn't have my mother's ashes and didn't see her body, I couldn't accept her death for a long time. Whenever I heard footsteps in the middle of the night, I woke up thinking, "There's my mother!" When she didn't come home for years, I had to accept that she was gone. That's when I thought, "I wonder if she died at the Kondos."

I heard that Mr. Kondo, who was left all alone, became mentally unbalanced and passed away.

Six months after the bombing, two aunts visited us from Osaka, and we had a narrow escape. Although our house had been spared the fire, it was leaning badly. I said, "Please come in and rest." But they were scared and showed no inclination to enter. I put cups of cold barley tea on a tray and served it to them as they stood outside.

Even as we stood there, our house collapsed with roar. Looking back and forth from aunt to aunt, I trembled so severely my teeth chattered.

After our house was flattened, my sister and I were sent to our aunt's house in Kita Arima (Shimabara). My brothers moved to the house my father was still renting to receive treatment.

The wound on my father's back was hardened and the scar around

tears in the shelter. I also heard the voices of people calling loudly the names of their children and other missing family members.

The next day rice balls were served, but for we had no appetite. Hardly anyone ate them.

My younger brother had been going to Nagasaki Commercial School, but classes had been cancelled. His classroom became a weapons manufacturing plant. He was working there at the time of the bombing. Thanks to daily training, he threw himself instantly to the floor. However, numerous pieces of window glass shattered by the blast stuck into his back. The classmate working next to him died instantly because his abdomen was slashed open.

My brother was treated by coworkers and walked all the way home along the streetcar tracks. He arrived with a bandage wrapped all around him. On his way, survivors suffering from burns reached out to him saying, "Please, give me water! Water, please!" They grabbed his ankles. He said, "I'll get some water for you, so let me go." Then he ran away from them.

My father and younger brother went to Ikeda Hospital in Shimabara for treatment. On their way, the burns on my father's neck, back and legs where cucumber slices had been placed were covered with hundreds of white maggots. They rented a house in front of the hospital and concentrated on getting some treatment.

My mother has been missing since that day. She had wondered if the house at Iwakawa-machi had been damaged by the conventional air raid on August 1. She went to check on the house and take some eggplants and cucumbers from our farm to a friend's house near Sanno Shrine. It was not until September that I learned where she was and what happened to her.

give them water, so I went out to the garden and picked a cucumber. I peeled it and gave that to them.

If I had not finished peeling that last potato and had rushed out to see the parachute, I would have been in the same state as my cousins. In fact, if we had gone to the old house as planned to get more of our belongings, we would have been killed instantly because our house was in Iwakawa-machi, not more than 500 meters from the hypocenter.

My cousins failed to control themselves and drank lots of water from the well during the night. The next morning their faces and bodies were swollen up hard like big bladders. A few days later my oldest sister and her husband took them to the relief station at Michino-o Elementary School. On August 11, the younger one passed away, followed by the older one on the 17th.

My father was outside like my cousins. He was blown about two meters by the blast and dropped into the eggplant garden. He had been hunched over weeding a field in front of our house, so he had serious burns on his back.

Many houses near Sumiyoshi Shrine had thatched roofs. Fire spread from a storehouse to a main house, then from one house to the next through the whole area.

The house Teruko and her family were in was some distance from the others and had tile roofing on both the storehouse and the main house. They escaped the fire. Their house was the only one in the area that remained unburned. However, the inside was so damaged, the family went to a shelter.

We couldn't enter the shelter because of the intense stench of burns and corpses. I could see survivors hugging each other, rejoicing with

Nagasaki August 9, 1945

their belongings little by little on a cart.

We planned to take more stuff to the new house on August 9, but we were so tired we decided to air out the clothes we had brought out previously.

I was peeling potatoes in the kitchen for lunch. My sixth grade cousin and his older brother (who was in high school) said, "A parachute is coming down!" I thought, "That'll be coming down slow." I continued peeling a potato until it was finished. Just as I was about to leave the house to see the parachute, a sulfur smell and blue smoke drifted in. I hurriedly turned back into the house and grabbed the edge of the door into a space down in our earthen floor.

I saw no light and heard no sound. The shock was so strong I had no idea what could possibly have happened. When I looked around, I saw all the glass windows broken and the inside of our house a chaotic jumble.

I was so terrified my legs wouldn't support me. I couldn't stand up so I crawled out. I found the two boys who had called to me earlier about the parachute. They had been transformed into the most grotesque figures. Their clothes were burnt, and they were half naked. Their faces, arms and other places where their skin had been exposed were badly burnt. The skin had peeled right off showing the bare red flesh below.

A firefighter was going around saying, "Don't give water to the ones with burns!"

I took the boys into the house and attempted to lay them down, but they had burns all over their bodies so they couldn't lay down. I had them sit down on the earthen floor and tried to give them some sort of treatment. They kept saying, "I need water!" I knew I shouldn't

Without my mother's ashes I can't believe she's dead.

Teruko Yamaguchi
Born October 1928. Exposed to the atomic bombing at her house below Sumiyoshi Shrine, 1.8 kilometers from the hypocenter. Her mother was killed by the bombing at a friend's house. Her father had gruesome burns on his back. Her brother's back was full of glass fragments. After the war ended, the four children reopened the laundry their parents had run. Married at 18, blessed with six children. Eighty-six years old, resides in Heiwa-machi, Nagasaki City.

We children scratched our father's "unbearably itchy" burn scars.

Teruko's parents ran a laundry in Iwakawa-machi. As the war got worse, food was strictly controlled by a ration system. Her parents bought a house with rice fields and gardens beneath Sumiyoshi Shrine. They had Teruko and her sister running the shop while they grew potatoes and rice for food. The shop was managed by Teruko (16), her older sister, and a hired cleaner.

Teruko was the seventh of nine children; four boys and five girls. The second and third sons were fighting in Burma. The second daughter was married and living in Shanghai. Teruko lived in the house beneath Sumiyoshi Shrine with a large family, including her parents, her other siblings, two of her oldest sister's children, and two cousins (her mother's late sister's children).

An intense air raid took place on August 1. Thinking it was dangerous to keep the laundry going, they decided to move to the house under the shrine. Beginning in early August, they transported

hospital tomorrow and stay there a few days." She was admitted to her regular hospital the next day.

The evening of May 30, my mother suddenly said, "I'd like to eat some watermelon." This was highly unusual. She was not the type to ask for something outrageous. It was not melon season, but I went to look for it anyway.

I found a watermelon after some struggle and brought it to her. She was overjoyed and held it in her mouth. "It's too early, isn't it? It's not very sweet." She screwed her eyebrows into wrinkles. Still, I felt relieved to see her eating a piece of watermelon.

"See you tomorrow!" I called out as I left the room. She said, "Good night," and put her hand up with a smile when I turned around at the door to look at her. That was the last time I saw her alive.

> Coming back to my hometown
> for the first time in years
> I glimpsed my mother
> in the motions of my children and their children
> Yasuko

learned it was not my father who left my mother. My mother proposed the divorce and forcefully took the action. I learned that from a *waka*.

> Looking at snows
> tossed about the sky
> from my bed
> I think about being
> a wife on my own.

At the end of WWII, tuberculosis was said to be incurable. Everyone was afraid of it because it was so contagious. And patients absolutely had to find some way to get nutritious food. So families couldn't afford to have a tubercular patient, no matter how rich they were.

My father tried hard to feed my mother nutritious food. He even sold all his property. My mother knew her illness would require a long treatment, so she rejected his help and resolved to divorce. She must have been thinking that she didn't want her disease to ruin his life. I am amazed by my mother's love for my father and her desire to spare him when she contracted a disease that would never heal.

> The morning I put on
> the lipstick I bought just in case,
> a letter arrived from my ex-husband.

There must have been many nights when she wept quietly in her bed. I am sure she deplored her illness, but I believe she never regretted the divorce, which she willingly gave him.

My mother's last moment came in May 1978. Happily sipping a cup of tea I served her she said, "I feel a bit tired, Yasuko. I'll go to the

However, my mother pushed back. "You can marry whoever you wish, as long as you're in love." The next year we received a Notice of Marriage from my younger brother, who was taken from me when I was two. My father had remarried and his new wife said, "What about meeting your sister once before you get married?" She sent me the notice.

My mother rejected that idea saying, "I'm not the one who raised him so I have no right to see him." But I persuaded her. "If you don't see him now, you'll never see him at all." We decided to go and see my brother, who was living in Nagoya.

Using the excuse of visiting my grandfather, who was ill, we met my brother in a hospital in Nagasaki. I don't know why, but I have no memory of my mother's behavior or my brother's attitude at that time. However, I do definitely remember thinking that I was absolutely sure he was really my brother, even though I was meeting him for the first time in such a long time.

That was the only time Yasuko's mother ever saw her son. The next time they met was at her funeral. Yasuko says she felt it was a good thing she forced her to see him. She also met her father at her mother's funeral. There, Yasuko learned that her parents' were six years apart in age and a few other facts like that. She learned more from her brother. Her father had moved to Yokohama thinking, "It's not good for my son and daughter to live in a small town like Nagasaki." He was looking for a new job through the shipping company he worked for in Nagasaki. He remarried in Yokohama.

My mother started to compose waka in the sanatorium. She left a large collection of her *waka* written in smooth, beautiful characters. It was only when I read her diary and *waka* after she passed away that I

impossible by bad health, either mine or my mother's. When that happened, I wrote letters. I wrote about my friends, my grandparents, anything that occurred to me, then sent the letter to my mother.

My mother would correct my writing and send it back to me. That made me so happy I wrote again and again. Eventually, I started writing essays and sent those to her as well. This exchange of letters with my mother taught me the joy of writing. Because of those efforts and her training, I received many awards in essay contests.

Around 1960 Yasuko's mother decided to undergo a revolutionary operation to remove one of her lungs—the whole lung with the ribs. The survival rate for this operation was estimated at 60 percent, but her mother was determined to gamble on a cure. The following year, her mother returned home having survived the operation and 12 years in a sanatorium.

It was unbelievable to me. I still remember well the night I slept with my mother for the first time in my grandparent's house in Isahaya. I was a junior high student, and I was already as tall as my mother. We laid futon next to each other and just talked and talked endlessly.

I graduated from high school. Then, when I was 22, a few years after starting work for a local bank, my infant tuberculosis recurred, this time in the form of renal tuberculosis. I quit the bank job and had one of my kidneys removed.

In 1972 when I was 27 I met my future husband. We decided to marry, but my grandfather forcefully opposed our marriage. He said, "Yasuko, you are an only child. You should marry a man we can adopt to succeed me in the Kunitake family!" He began looking for an appropriate son-in-law.

divorced my mother when she was ill."

To tell the truth, I, too, was in bad shape. I easily tired and often fell ill with anemia. At school, when morning assembly was prolonged even a little, everything would go black, and I would have to sit down on the spot. During physical education class and sports days, I was an observer. After a while I contracted infant tuberculosis and had to get streptomycin injections in my buttocks every day. Eventually, I dropped out of school for a year.

Only thing I always looked forward to was going to see my mother in Nagasaki. Usually once a month, my grandfather would take me from Isahaya by bus. We went up a small hill to the sanatorium, walking up a long slope from the bus stop. I was so happy and got so excited thinking, "I'm going to see my mother!"

My mother was in a room with six female patients. I used to take walks with her in the woods on the sanatorium grounds. I sang her all the songs I learned at school. One day she laughed and said, "You're tone-deaf because I'm tone-deaf." I didn't feel offended at all. I was just happy to be like my mother.

There was a peculiarly large and eerie building on the grounds of the Tagami sanatorium. It was the crematory. Out of fear of contagion, all patients who died in the sanatorium were cremated in that building.

Once, my grandmother patted me on the head saying, "If only there'd been no war and no atomic bomb.... If only your mother hadn't fallen so ill. I wouldn't have to look on such a pitiful mother and child." She had tears in her eyes.

The meetings with my mother I enjoyed so much were often made

In the midst of confusion and chaos, her mother was informed that her grandfather, who lived in Nagasaki, was missing. The next day she went out with her mother-in-law to look for him. Yasuko's mother walked with her big belly from her house near Suwa Shrine straight through the hypocenter area to her relative's house in Iwakawa-machi. Neither she nor her mother-in-law had any idea about something called "radiation." They went into hypocenter on their own.

My grand-grandfather eventually came home, but he soon began complaining about his health. He died of an unknown illness in June the next year.

My mother had been one of the healthiest children around. She never took a single day off from school, from elementary school right through girls' high school. But two days after she delivered me, she felt weak. When she delivered my brother in January 1948 she suffered extreme anemia, heart problems, hypotension and eventually contracted tuberculosis.

After struggling at home, she went to a tuberculosis sanatorium in Tagami for long-term treatment.

My newborn brother was heir to succeed my father, so he was taken to live with our father's family. Not yet three years old, I was taken to my mother's parent's house in Isahaya. The two of us lived completely separate lives after that.

I grew up not knowing my father. By the time I was old enough to understand the situation, my parents were divorced, and my mother was in the sanatorium. I never had a conversation about my father with my mother. She never mentioned him. I didn't ask about him. However, over the years I always held a deep anger at "my father who

Nagasaki August 9, 1945

My mother consigned her pain and grief to *waka* (31-syllable poem).

Yasuko Tasaki
Born in November 1945. Exposed to the atomic bombing at her house in Nishiyama-machi, three kilometers from the hypocenter. She was a seven-month fetus. Her parents divorced when she was a toddler. She became a good writer by exchanging letters with her mother, who was in a tuberculosis sanitarium. Received numerous awards in essay contests. Because of recurring of infant tuberculosis, developed renal tuberculosis. Married at 27. Sixty-nine years old; resides in Eisho Higashi-machi, Isahaya City.

My anger at my father for divorcing my ill mother was swept away by our reunion.

I am an in-utero survivor. My Atomic Bomb Survivor Health Book states:

"Age at exposure – fetus" "Place of exposure – Shimo Nishiyama-machi, Nagasaki City, three kilometers from hypocenter" "Situation immediately after exposure – entered hypocenter area in mother's womb; mother was looking for grand-grandfather who had gone to Iwakawa-machi, one kilometer from hypocenter."

My mother (Nuiko Kunitake) was 20; I had been in her womb for 7 months. The air-raid warning was cleared. My mother was sewing baby clothes for me, chatting with her mother-in-law.

Yasuko later heard that "a lightning-like flash ran through the sky, followed by tremendous roar. A cabinet, other furniture and a beam from the ceiling fell down. Your mother protected her fetus, instinctively laying down on her stomach."

Masaki got married in 1957. His wife was two year older than him and came from Futsu-cho. They were blessed with two daughters and have had a happy marriage. He got prostate cancer when he was 73, but got over it.

Among my best memories are the times my wife would put our very small daughter on her back, then get onto the back of my motorbike and we would ride into downtown Nagasaki on my days off.

Because I was blown into a reservoir, I could easily have died that day. And yet, here I am, still alive. I'm deeply grateful for this. I decided to tell my A-bomb story for future generations primarily on behalf of the many classmates at Shiroyama Elementary School who have gone before me.

chest and belly looked like a turtle stomach (lower shell). The scabs all over them became extremely itchy. I could hardly stand it.

By November that year, my scabs were nearly gone, and I received notice that my school would reopen. I went to school and found out that nearly all my classmates were dead. Of the 1500 students that had been enrolled at Shiroyama Elementary School, fewer than 100 survived.

We began receiving lessons in a room rented from Inasa Elementary School, which was located three kilometers from our school. The following spring all 6th graders graduated. We graduates numbered 14.

That summer, my oldest sister who had stayed at our uncle's house in Kawara-machi, died of A-bomb disease. Another older sister who had had no injury at all died of leukemia in 1951.

In 1968, 23 years after the bombing, the first Shiroyama Elementary School reunion was organized by a TV station. The fourteen who had graduated together were down to nine. Classmates continued to die year after year; there are scarcely any of us left today.

If I were asked for memories of Shiroyama Elementary School, I would have to say that lessons stopped even before summer holiday and we mostly had days off. Thus, I really have very few memories. One thing I do recall is that our schoolyard turned into a farm. I clearly remember growing peas and potatoes.

When he was 17, thanks to a recommendation from a neighbor, he got a job of doing road construction work for City Hall. Soon he became a City Hall employee and worked there 44 years until retirement. After retirement, he was reemployed as a security guard in the main office of Nagasaki City Hall. He worked there another six years.

instead of a bandage. They put it on my stomach like a waistband, tying it behind my back. This was a terrible mistake. The cloth became solid with bloody pus and adhered to my wounds. It was nearly impossible to peel off. They soaked it in water starting at the edge and peeled it off slowly during the next three days. The skin from my chest to my belly peeled completely off after all. A liquid oozed from my bare red flesh, but we decided to let my skin dry out naturally without any bandage.

Strangely, I didn't feel much pain or sorrow. I had no feeling to see the bodies of my friends. I think my nerves were just completely paralyzed.

Masaki's father thought it was too pitiful to lay him down virtually on the ground outside, though he was in the three tatami mat space. He was temporarily moved to his father's brother's house in Kawara-machi. His two older sisters were already being cared for at their uncle's house, so he was transported there. Two months later, Masaki's father, who had some carpentry skills, built a shack out of scraps from their crushed house. Masaki returned to this two six -mat room shack.

Soon after the bombing, I struggled not only with the burns from chest to belly but also with chronic diarrhea and the loss of my hair. My father bought Chinese herbal medicine for me that cost 50 yen (equivalent to $500 today). He had me take it saying, "Don't waste this valuable medicine." It was bitter and difficult to drink but it had marvelous effects. It was expensive so I took it only once a day, but first my diarrhea and hair loss stopped, then my consciousness grew clear again. I didn't apply any ointment, and yet my chest and belly improved rapidly, making scabs. My burns began to improve. Still, my

moaning. I crawled out, found a dry streambed in front of the shelter, and lay there for two days.

After a while, my father came looking for me. As soon as he found me, he scolded me, saying, "I told you to come to the field. Why didn't you come?"

My father had cultivated some land on a mountain to plant potatoes. I had gone to help him the day before, but the day of the bombing, my friends came by my house so I went swimming.

Later, I learned that my mother was unconscious. A beam in our collapsed house had hit her head.

My father collected usable pillars and beams from our broken house and leaned them against trees in front of our house. He made a space about as big enough to lay three tatami mats and let me lay down there. My burns suppurated, with pus oozing from the open wounds.

We had lots of bees that summer. Bees flew over to drink my pus. When I drove them away, they stung me before leaving. That was quite painful, so I couldn't really drive away bees or flies. As a result, I was soon infested with maggots. Maggots crawling around my wounds and bees coming to drink my pus—I was a living corpse. I was completely miserable.

My big toe was fixed tightly with relative ease. They rubbed it with potato vines. However, the burns from my chest to belly were much harder to cure than I expected.

About a week after the bombing, a relief station was created in an open space on the grounds of Shiroyama Elementary School. Masaki's father carried him on his back to the school. Finally, he was able to get something like medical treatment.

They put a kind of oil on my burns, then used a big triangular cloth

burns. Also, I had turned my face away, so it was spared. However, I did have burns on my head, my belly, my arms and legs.

My chest felt too hot. I put my hand where it hurt, and the skin stuck to my hand. Much of the skin on my chest peeled right off. My clothes were burnt to tatters, and the skin on my arms had nearly all peeled off. When I looked up the bank, I saw only two or three of my ten friends. I heard later that seven of us died in less than a week.

Masaki staggered home alone from the reservoir to his house in Shiroyama. On his way, he saw houses flattened as if they had been stamped on. These smashed houses lined the road. So much debris was scattered around he could hardly find places to step. He often didn't even know if he was walking on the ground or on smashed roofs.

I finally got home, but my house was knocked over by the blast. I couldn't find a way in. I stood in a daze in front of my house feeling the strength draining out of me. People barely able to move took refuge in a shelter near my house. I started walking toward the shelter. I had been walking barefoot, and all of a sudden, I couldn't walk anymore. I looked down at my feet and found the base of my right big toe split open. The toe was just dangling, almost torn off.

I held my big toe on and, crawling, I made it to the shelter. Some others came crawling in by themselves. Others came in on someone's back or in someone's arms. The survivors in our shelter were pitiful—one in particular. His eyeballs were nearly out of their sockets leaving big holes open on his face. Two days later, his eyeball sockets were full of maggots wriggling in and out through the holes in the sockets.

Another one had glass shards piercing her whole body. There was nothing any of us could do to help. I couldn't stand the smell and

Nagasaki August 9, 1945

Shiroyama Elementary School's 1,500 students were reduced to 100.

Masaki Morimoto
Born April 1933. Exposed to the atomic bombing while swimming in a reservoir in Shiroyama-machi, 1.2 kilometers from the hypocenter. He was 12. He was one of fewer than 100 of the approximately 1500 students at Shiroyama Elementary School who survived. Eighty-two years old, resides in Yanagidani-machi, Nagasaki City.

I want to tell my A-bomb story for my classmates.

That morning about nine o'clock, Masaki Morimoto, a 6th grader at Shiroyama Elementary School, went to a nearby reservoir to swim with 10 friends in his neighborhood. It was already a hot, humid day, so all ten boys were swimming in skimpy loincloths.

We were about to go home. We had been swimming excitedly so we were tired and hungry. Some were putting on shirts and trousers. A few of us were about to climb up to the top of the bank when a 5th grader pointed up at the sky and yelled, "Wow, a parachute bomb! Look at that!"

Others ran up the bank saying, "What is it?" A strange three-umbrella parachute was riding on the wind coming closer and closer out of the sky over the Nagasaki Shipyard. When it was right above the wooded area near us, everything turned pure white and I lost consciousness. I remember feeling as if I were in a white cloud.

When I came to, I was in the reservoir. I must have been blown down the bank and into the water. I was quite lucky to have fallen into the water. My body was instantly soaked in water, which countered the

years until retirement. At 30 I married a man I was introduced to by an acquaintance. He had come from Kumamoto Prefecture and was working for a fruit and vegetable company. He was 10 years older than me and cared for me very well.

When I was pregnant with our first daughter, I was a bit nervous. But then I heard my husband said, "I wonder if our baby will be born with a long toe or something. I want a baby with no defects." I knew he was worried about the effects of the bombing.

We have two daughters. When our first daughter was in elementary school, she had a health checkup, and the doctor said, "You have a tendency toward anemia." When she's healthy, I don't worry much. But when she has any kind of problem, I can't help thinking, "Maybe this is because of…" I hate thinking like this.

On the day of the bombing, I knew nothing at all about radiation. Otherwise we would not have gone to the ruins of the dormitory in Komaba-cho near the hypocenter immediately after the bombing. I first learned about "entry exposure" when I heard that soldiers who had entered the hypocenter to clear debris developed diseases of unknown origin. They were sent to University Hospital and many died.

I didn't know how to interpret this information, so I made myself believe that radiation doesn't all happen right away; it comes out over time. When we went to the hypocenter immediately after the bombing, the radioactive gas had yet to be fully generated. I don't know if this makes any scientific sense, but without believing this, I would not have been able to confront with my fate.

Nagasaki August 9, 1945

The victims I saw near the Mitsubishi Steel Works were dead. I had a feeling similar to submission; I didn't care that much. But here, people were screaming and struggling desperately. I couldn't help but feel terribly sorry for them, but there was nothing we could do. We just kept walking silently toward Togitsu.

We finally reached Togitsu in the middle of the night. We had not eaten anything since noon. The villagers gave us some rice balls, and I still remember how good they tasted. We were taken into a big house. When I was able to lie down under a mosquito net, I finally felt a sense of relief.

The next day, they said, "Those who came from Shimabara should go home." I went to Michino-o Station. Again, I saw a lot of injured people in the square behind the station, and their numbers increased even as I watched.

One person's clothes were tattered and full of blood. Another's hair had taken the shape of the helmet he wore, and his exposed ears and neck were burnt badly. It was so grotesque, I had to turn my eyes away.

I asked and was allowed to ride the train, but I failed to get home that day. I spent the night in the train at Shimabara Station, arriving at my home in Kazusa the next day.

My mother told me the family had been saying, "Fusae must be dead." "How can we find her body?" The family told me they could see the mushroom cloud from Kazusa, and Nagasaki had burned all night.

Many of my friends died. Many of those who survived initially died in the torments of A-bomb diseases. Nearly all survivors live in anxiety knowing they could be inflicted with disorders at any time.

I took lessons in dressmaking in Kazusa. When I was 20, I returned to Nagasaki with my friend. I worked for an insurance company for 26

The food in Shimabara where I grew up was not that bad, so eating the gruel mixed with soybean dregs and weeds the dormitory served was painful to me.

Three women lived together in a six tatami mat room. On days off we all hung our wash in the yard. We had a dorm mother and a superintendent, but they supervised all 10 houses. I didn't even know where they lived.

When I arrived at what I assumed were the ruins of our dormitory, all 10 houses had vanished. Even the trees around the dormitories were completely burned to the ground. I could see Shiroyama Elementary School and Chinzei Gakuin Junior High School up on the mountainside. I used these two schools as landmarks in my effort to confirm where my dormitory had stood.

A number of other residents who worked for the Ordnance Works came back to those ruins, but no one said a word. I heard later that our housemother and superintendent were reduced to skeletons where they sat in their chairs. All who had been in the dormitory preparing for the night shift were killed instantly.

As I stood there in a daze, a person with an armband saying "subsection chief, Mitsubishi" said, "This area is dangerous. You should go to Togitsu (a town north of Nagasaki)." I had just come to Nagasaki four months earlier and had no idea where Togitsu was. Of the 10 of us standing there, one knew where Togitsu was. We walked off following her.

When we came to Ohashi Bridge next to Komaba-cho, most of the bridge was blown away leaving only the naked iron frame spanning the river. We crawled cross that bridge frame. Looking down, I saw a crowd of injured victims who had come to the river seeking water. They were groaning and begging for help. Many fell into the river; many of those were washed away.

Nagasaki August 9, 1945

It took me two hours to get to the dormitory, and it was gone without a trace. The whole area was a burnt plain as far as I could see. A few fellow workers who had arrived before me were trying to get their bearings. "Weren't we about here?" Everything was so completely changed.

Our dormitory was a one-story house in a row of about ten similar houses standing together. Residents lived in these houses by company. That is, shipyard workers shared one house, ordnance workers shared another, and so on. As I recall, 100 to 200 young women lived in those dormitories. They came from Goto Islands and the Shimabara Peninsula. Some had graduated from school; others were labor service volunteers from girls' schools. Those girls were going to a large facility in Maruo-machi every other day to study. I was among those who went to study.

We studied every other day, but every day we first went to our workplaces in the morning at the regular time, then headed for Maruo-machi. When an air-raid warning sounded while we were studying at Maruo-machi, we were supposed to take refuge in a nearby shelter. When studying, I felt differently about the warnings than when I was at work. I didn't go to the shelter when the alarms sounded because I was so used to hearing them near the end of my study sessions. I was especially reluctant when it was hot.

Fusae left the dormitory at seven in the morning and commuted to the shipyard; she returned in the evening. Her workplace didn't have a night shift, but some companies did. The dorms had commuting cooks by company and all the residents ate in a single dining hall.

chief when I heard an enormous explosion. The glass in the windows of two separate walls broke at the same time, and the shattered glass flew toward me. I was well trained to hit the floor quickly, and I made myself wear a long sleeve blouse despite the heat of summer, so I was lucky and had no injury. Everyone in the office was shocked and rushed to be the first one into the shelter. I went down the stairs being pushed by the crowd all the way to a shelter. There I saw people covered in blood due to flying glass but I didn't see any with burns.

The previous day in the elevator I had seen a co-worker in the Drawing Section with his arm in a sling. I asked, "What happened?" He replied, "I went to Hiroshima for a business trip and it was hit by a new type bomb!" That meant he had encountered two atomic bombings.

Fusae stayed in the shelter near her office until evening. Thinking, "It must be ok by now," she went out to find a sea of fire on the other side of the river (near the prefectural government buildings). She couldn't imagine what had happened.

Her dormitory was in Komaba-machi near the hypocenter. She tried to get back there, but all transportation was stopped. Normally, she would have taken a boat from Mizunoura, where the shipyard was, to Ohato, then go back to the dormitory by streetcar.

With no sign of any boats or streetcars, she decided to walk through Inasa to her dormitory. She left the shelter around 5:00 in the evening and arrived at the dormitory after 7:00.

The further she advanced into the city, the more badly damaged the houses were. When she entered the area near Mitsubishi Steel Works, charred corpses were everywhere. Streetcar rails were lifted and bent like a bows toward the sky. The Steel Works buildings were nothing but skeletons.

Nagasaki August 9, 1945

Entered the city right after the bombing with no idea about radiation.

Fusae Fukushita
Born September 1930. Exposed to the atomic bombing at Mizunoura Mitsubishi Shipyard, three kilometers from the hypocenter when she was 14. Learned dressmaking in Kazusa (now, Minami Shimabara City); came back to Nagasaki when she was 20. Worked for an insurance company until retirement. Married at 30, blessed by two daughters. Eighty-four years old, resides in Nameshi, Nagasaki City.

Those who survived died early, tormented by A-bomb diseases.

Fusae Fukushita graduated from post-elementary school in Shimabara Peninsula and entered Kazusa Youth School in her neighborhood. She was one of only two students from that school assigned to a munitions company in Nagasaki. Employed as an apprentice, she moved to a dormitory. Fusae went to school one day and Mizunoura Mitsubishi Shipyard the next. She was apprenticed to learn drawing, but had many miscellaneous tasks. One was to go to the dining hall in the next building around 11 am to get lunch and bring it back for her section chief. She usually received some bread and a side dish, bringing them back to her section. A classmate was assigned to the Ordnance Works at Tategami.

I had come four months earlier to Nagasaki from Kazusa. That day I was on the 6th floor of the office building of Shipyard. At 11 o'clock I had just started walking toward the exit to get lunch for my section

Because of that experience, I went to the even better equipped university hospital for my third delivery (second daughter). However, the baby stayed in the birth canal too long. She was born unconscious and not breathing. I felt so sorry for her and apologized to her, crying, "I'm sorry my pushing was so weak! Please, please don't die!"

The nurse slapped the baby many times and finally she let out her first cry. When I heard her voice, I was so happy I almost jumped out of the bed to hold her.

The atomic bomb is especially cruel to women. Some were denied marriage because they were survivors. Others gave up on marriage or if they got married they gave up on children because of the rumor that they would give birth to deformed babies. Many who got pregnant and endured nine months of hell due to anxiety. And, like Mitsuko, many risked their lives each time they gave birth. The atomic bomb inflicts terrible suffering on women, whose natural role is to nurture new life.

the baby's health than I was joyful about becoming a mother. It was agony every day. What if my baby were deformed? I was exposed outside, unshielded. Anything could happen. I thought the same things again and again in circles, and my thoughts grew darker and darker. I couldn't sleep at night. I lost my appetite. All I did was pray continually that my baby would be born with no defect.

When the time came I was still in a state of high anxiety. I delivered in January 1965 at a private clinic. The doctor was a woman, so I immediately grabbed her and asked, "Is there anything abnormal about my child? Does it have five fingers and toes?"

She replied, "You have a healthy boy." The anxiety that had bothered me so much melted away immediately. But since I had been so anxious for so long, I felt all the strength in my body drain out of me, and my joy was short-lived. Eight hours after delivery, I felt something clammy below the waist. I was hemorrhaging badly.

When I had been going to the A-bomb Hospital, I had been worried about anemia. Now, I was diagnosed with "leukemia and hemophilia, characterized by an increase in red blood cells." Immediately they prepared a blood transfusion. I was attached to a tube and stayed in the clinic for more than a week.

Despite my poor overall health, my breasts swelled normally, and I experienced the great joy of motherhood holding my son in my arm as he nursed eagerly.

Mitsuko was saved from death by a blood transfusion after her first delivery, but she confronted crises with each subsequent birth. She chose the well-equipped city hospital for her second birth (first daughter), but again, she suffered massive bleeding and was in critical condition due to anemia.

by evening. My only break was taking firewood to my relative's house where they let me take a bath. Soothing my little siblings as they cried for their mother, I wanted to cry myself. To make matters even more unbearable, my relationship with my stepfather's mother was bad and got worse as time went by.

Her uncle on her father's side was living in Nagasaki and felt sorry for Mitsuko. He invited her to Nagasaki. Although she was worried about leaving her siblings, she knew she was at the edge physically and emotionally. She decided to leave the house, trusting the children to her stepfather's mother.

Just when I thought, "Finally, I can start my own life," I started going to the A-bomb Hospital regularly. My exposure and too much hard work had given me extreme anemia. I got tired easily and often got dizzy just standing up. It was hard even to get to the hospital.

When I reached that age, my uncle brought me an offer of marriage. However, I had heard the rumor that A-bomb survivors have deformed babies, so I had decided I would never marry. But when I was 27, my uncle pushed me very hard, so I got married to an electrical engineer. Soon after we got married, my husband's mother, who lived in Saga, visited us. She had heard something about me and asked directly, "You were in the atomic bombing, weren't you?" I admitted it honestly. My mother-in-law said nothing, but I could see in her face that she was upset.

I thought my husband would say something about it that night, but he didn't. I don't know if his mother didn't tell him or if she told him but he didn't mention it. Therefore I left it alone. I never told my husband that I am an A-bomb survivor.

When I was pregnant with my first child I was more nervous about

Nagasaki August 9, 1945

I was called a "red spider lily." My hair didn't grow back for a long time, and when it finally came in, it was kinky, sort of dancing on my head. I was ashamed and sad, a miserable young girl.

Her mother remarried soon after Mitsuko went back to school. Her stepfather was the husband of her late aunt (her mother's younger sister.) He lost his wife and three daughters so he was alone. He returned from the Philippines to his house on Hisaka Island. Mitsuko liked him very much. Her mother had declared she would never marry again, but seeing Mitsuko being so happy with him, and he with her, she decided to marry him.

They had four boys and girls under me. But then one day, my mother suddenly fell ill while working on the farm. She passed away on the way to the hospital in Fukue. Her youngest child was still nursing. It had been 10 years since the bombing, but the cause was A-bomb disease.

I was 18 at the time. I had a stepfamily from my mother's remarriage, but in a sense, I was suddenly truly alone. Worse yet, my stepfather developed gangrene and couldn't move. I was forced to take care of my four younger siblings and do all the housework. Plus, I had to do the farm work my mother had done.

I dropped my two brothers off at nursery school and pulled the 3-year old by his hand. I put the nursing baby and lunchbox together in a big basket and carried them on my back. I took them with me to the potato field or the rice field. I had the 3-year old boy watch the baby while I planted seedlings or potato cuttings. I had no milk, of course, so I softened some potatoes in my mouth and fed that to the baby. I was literally their surrogate mother.

The days wore on. I worked so hard I was completely exhausted

pressed me down saying, "You have to bear this, Mitsuko! This is your only hope for ever walking normally!" For years, I shivered with fright just hearing the word "massage." But I am extremely grateful to my mother. Thanks to her, I am able to walk.

After the atomic bombing, Mitsuko and her mother lived with her uncle (her late father's older brother) on Hisaka, one of the Goto Islands. When they arrived on that island, Mitsuko was barely conscious. She looked like a corpse. Her hair had fallen out; she was nothing but skin and bone. All she did was moan, "I'm dying! It's killing me!" Seeing her in such agony everyone said, "She'd suffer less if she could just die quickly." People around her were always thinking, "Will it be today or tomorrow?" But Mitsuko clung to life.

I was confined to bed. I couldn't even go to the bathroom without my mother holding me like a baby. One day when I had finished a bowel movement and we were on our way back from the yard to my room, still being supported by my mother, something gushed out of my body.

My mother thought it was urine and scolded me. When we looked more carefully, a swelling in my groin had broken open and something like pus had poured out.

My mother later said, "I wonder if the gas you breathed from atomic bomb collected there."

The scar from that wound is still a large indentation. I also had swellings on my knee and ankle. I had them cut and the pus discharged at a hospital. After that, I began improving quickly everyday. By April the next year I was ready to start the third grade again.

I entered an elementary school on Hisaka Island, but I was bullied.

Nagasaki August 9, 1945

to get my sister and bring her home. It had been decided that my uncle would adopt my sister, so she was frequently sent to his house. When my mother reached his house, it was gone. It was nothing but a heartbreaking mountain of smoldering debris filled with an unbearable stench. My mother looked desperately for my sister in the burnt ruins, but in vain.

It seems my sister was blown away by the blast and incinerated somewhere by the fire. My mother stuffed some earth from the ruins into a pot in lieu of her ashes. She brought the pot home.

Mitsuko's aunt (her mother's younger sister) was hanging out the wash in front of the house. She suffered serious burns from head to toe. Miraculously, she was still alive. Mitsuko's mother borrowed a cart from a neighbor and lay her completely burned sister in it. Then she put Mitsuko and her cousins in one corner of the cart. They headed for the relief station at Shin-kozen Elementary School.

That relief station was so full of injured victims there was no space even to step. But their house was gone, and they had lived in a shelter, so they stayed in the school.

My aunt's burn was so bad she had maggots crawling all over her. My mother would pick them out of her wounds one by one with a twig. My aunt soon died, and my mother cremated her own sister by herself. When my mother came home with my aunt's ashes, one of my cousins was dead. She had to go back to cremate her.

I was able to walk a little, but my right leg didn't bend at all. I crawled to move about the house. My mother often carried me on her back and took me to get massages. The massages on my rigid right leg were so painful I couldn't stand it. I cried and screamed, but my mother

My house was near Hachiman Shrine, a 15-minute walk to the school for us children. We went to school in a group, walking behind the school building. The roots from trees spread across this side lane, and when it rained the lane soon got muddy. It was quite a difficult walk on rainy days. When we arrived at school, older students would be watching us from the upstairs windows. They would shout, "Your arms were not swinging together, and you were not marching in time." They made us start over, marching in single file. That drove me crazy.

It was summer vacation. I was playing with my friends, two sisters from next door. I looked up as the airplanes flew over us. I saw them drop something black. The next instant, there was a tremendous flash, and we were blown off our feet by the blast.

A huge apricot tree fell over. I was lying on the ground with a root of that tree pressing down on my neck. I had serious burns over the right half of my body. The two sisters I had been playing with were trapped by tree's branches. All three of us managed to get away from that tree and take refuge on the mountainside.

The mountain soon filled with people taking refuge there. Many didn't even look like human beings. Their arms and chests were burnt and covered with reddish sores. Mitsuko and her two friends went to a shelter, but it was full. They sat down by a spring that trickled by in front of the shelter. They waited for daybreak.

The next morning, one of the sisters was dead. Ninety-three percent of the students enrolled at Shiroyama Elementary School died in the atomic bombing.

My mother had been at Mitsubishi Steel Works and fled to an evacuation site in Nagayo. The next day, she went to my uncle's house

Nagasaki August 9, 1945

Atomic bombs show no mercy to women. Mothers carrying babies were tormented to the end.

Mitsuko Iwamoto
Born March 1937. Exposed to the atomic bombing near her house, 500 meters from the hypocenter. She was 8 and suffered serious burns. Her parents and sister died, leaving her completely alone. She suffered from extreme anemia but got married when she was 27. She survived three dangerous deliveries with heavy blood loss and near death of the baby. She is blessed with one boy and two girls. Seventy-eight years old. Resides in Menoto, Nagasaki City.

I never told my husband about my exposure.
During my pregnancy, I had many sleepless nights.

Mitsuko Iwamoto's father was a policeman. He had died while serving in Korea several years before the bombing. Her mother was raising Mitsuko (8) and her sister (6) while working for Mitsubishi Steel Works.

Mitsuko's aunt (her mother's younger sister) and her three daughters lived with them because her aunt's husband was a soldier serving in the Philippines.

I was a third grader at Shiroyama Elementary School. School events like school trips and sports meetings were cancelled. I have no fun memories of school. My classroom was on the 3rd floor. Whenever an air-raid warning sounded, we had to run down to the 1st floor to the shelter. My only memory is rushing down the stairs every time the warning sounded.

a child. Soon, I was pregnant. One day my husband said, "I've heard that atomic bomb survivors deliver black babies." I wondered where he had heard that rumor. Then he asked, "Are you a survivor?"

In that instant the memory of the atomic bombing 13 years earlier came flooding back, I was speechless. I have no idea how I answered him.

I knew he was asking not because he doubted me but because he was worried. Like all parents, he worried about having a healthy baby. I was painfully aware of his anxiety. Still, I had no choice but to keep hiding my exposure. If I had told him I was a survivor, he would have been even more anxious. I kept it to myself. However, I felt very guilty about not telling him. That guilt was worse than the anxiety about the baby. I had many sleepless nights.

My husband, who knew nothing about me and the A-bomb, was so kind and considerate when I was pregnant. He treated me like I was his treasure saying, "You just rest in bed."

To meet my husband's expectations, I prayed wholeheartedly for a healthy baby. I thought I would die if my baby were born black. During that time, I often thought about the fetus that died with my mother.

On March 23, 1959, the baby came with an unexpectedly easy delivery, given my health. That baby, born despite my emotional instability and internal conflict, was a healthy, chubby girl with normal white skin.

When I heard the wife of our landlord, who attended my delivery, say, "It's a beautiful girl! She resembles her father!" I was overwhelmed by joy. I sobbed out loud.

ugly. I have to admit that a person seeing him for the first time would be repulsed. I think that's why he gradually stopped going out. It seems the children in our neighborhood bullied him and called him "A-bomb kid".

Still, that brother got married in 1958 when he was 20. Now he is blessed with five children and is leading a happy life. However, he hides his scars by wearing long-sleeved shirts even in summer. And he never fails to wear gloves to hide the keloids running up his hands.

After graduating from junior high school, I got a job at a mandarin orange canning plant in Inasa. I was often too weak to work due to anemia. I didn't want to be a burden on the company so I quit. My physical condition was such that it took me two or three times as long to do household chores compared to a healthy housewife.

In 1958, the same year as my brother, I married a sardine fisherman after being introduced by a friend of my father. I was 22. I was quite anxious about my health, but I married without telling my husband about my A-bomb experience. In those days, rumor had it that a woman who inhaled the gas from the A-bomb would deliver deformed babies. In many cases, when a woman was found to be a survivor, she was divorced. I decided never to tell him, no matter what.

My honeymoon, which was supposed to be one of the happiest times of my life, brought me misery. Day after day I couldn't get out of bed because of dizziness and nausea. I wanted to cook for my husband. I got up and stood in the kitchen, but the blood drained from my head. Everything went black. I got dizzy and fell to the floor.

I went to a doctor who said, "You have extreme anemia. The cause is unknown."

Despite my poor health and instability, I very much wanted to have

Eventually Yuriyo's father got a job at Mitsubishi Shipyard through his brother's introduction. However, he began drinking more and more alcohol to distract himself from the loneliness and grief of having lost his wife. He started to drink in places other than home. He began missing work due to hangovers. After a few months, he was fired. It became increasingly difficult for the family to get by.

The year of the atomic bombing was a good one for summer oranges. My siblings and I stole oranges wherever we could. That was how we kept from starving.

Maybe because we were stealing oranges, whenever something was missing in my neighborhood, my neighbors immediately blamed me and my siblings. We all cried about this and said, "If our mother were here, we wouldn't be attacked like this."

My younger brother who had been terribly burned in the bombing got sores all over his body. His face was so swollen he couldn't even open his eyes. He was suffering and saying, "I can't see. I can't see. It's so painful!" His arms and the backs of his hands were infested with maggots. Bloody pus oozed out of the sores, the suppuration hollowed out his flesh and smelled terrible.

I had heard that potato juice was good for burns, so I started visiting our relatives in Sotome to get potatoes. I grated them and applied the juice to my brother's burns. Whenever I put juice on him he shrieked, "It stings!" "It hurts!" I felt so sorry for him, but thanks to the potatoes, he was doing fairly well in a year and a half. He returned to elementary school having missed two years.

However, the keloid scars on his head and down onto his face were

Nagasaki August 9, 1945

Yuriyo's burnt brother (7), her youngest brother (5) and youngest sister (3) stayed at her uncle's house at Sotome for some time. The four older siblings had to live by themselves in the broken-down house in Inasa. They had no electricity or water. Like Hiroshima's many street children, they lived a harsh life. They managed to survive by going out, each with a different group, to look for food. When things got too bad, her oldest sister or brother went to their uncle's house at Sotome and got some sweet potatoes. It was difficult to make fire at home, so they just washed and ate them raw.

The water system at our house was broken so my oldest brother told me to go out and get water from a tap in the ruins. I went out, and there was a man standing in front of our house. The man stared at me and said, "Are you Yuriyo?" It was my father. My father had come back from the bloody battlefields of Saipan. We had heard the Japanese were totally defeated there, so we were amazed.

Besides, he looked like a different man. He had a beard and a sword at his side. He wore a combat cap and looked like a general. Rather than joy, fear and surprise came first.

My father asked, "Where's your mother?"

I replied, "She's dead." He didn't say anything. He just looked down and stood still. After a while, he burst into tears, as if a dam inside him had broken. He was screaming, "I will kill all those big-noses from the US! Give me back my wife!"

Yuriyo's father repaired their tilted house. When they ran out of food, he went to his brother's house in Sotome and got potatoes to give the children something to eat. That miserable life continued for over a year.

soothe him along the way and finally arrived at my uncle's house.

As soon as we arrived, my mother said, "I'm worried about our house in Inasa." She went back to take care of the damaged house. She must have breathed in a lot of radioactive gas. When the four of us older children went home to Inasa a few days later, black spots had appeared on my mother's face. Those spots spread day after day to her entire body. Her lips turned purple. She kept gulping water saying, "I'm tired! I'm tired!" Then, on August 16th a week after the bombing, she died, pregnant with her 8th child.

Right before she died she kept saying, "Just a small amount would be fine, but I want to eat white rice." "I don't want to die. Where's my husband? Hasn't he come back yet?" She grasped my hand and opened her eyes so wide it seemed her eyeballs would jump out, and died. She was 33 years old. She was a fair-skinned, small and silent woman.

My uncle and four of us cremated my mother's corpse early in the afternoon the next day. My uncle didn't want to let us see him lighting the fire under my mother. He told us to stay away. After a while, when the fire was burning, he called us to him.

I was so sad to see my mother's body burning, and it was frightening as well. We kept piling on the wood to make the burning go faster. It probably took three or four hours. I remember it took quite a long time. We picked some ashes and remaining bone and put them into a broken bowl we had found in the rubble. What had been my mother's body several hours earlier was now just a bowlful of ash and bone.

When we came back to my uncle's house holding the ashes in a bowl, my younger brothers and sisters asked, "Where did Mommy go?" "When will she be back?" My oldest sister sobbed and squeezed them tight but remained silent.

saccharin instead of sugar. In those days we hardly ever got sweets, so even a single mouthful of sweet bean soup per person was a great treat. We were eagerly looking forward to it being ready.

Finally, my mother said, "It's ready, but it's hot, so I'll let you eat it later when it cools down." In that instant, the flash struck us, followed by a tremendous booooming blast.

The house tilted over but stayed standing. My mother, my siblings and I were all blown off our feet by the blast. The sweet bean soup flew in all directions. I could see straight out of the house and saw lots of clothes flying through the air like kites.

The brother just younger than me (7) was taking a nap on the veranda. He was seriously burned all over his body. Looking for someplace cool, I had been lying next to him. But as the sun came up, it got hot on veranda so I woke up and went inside the house. My brother had especially terrible burns on his face and arms. My mother was distraught when she saw him so grotesquely transformed.

My oldest sister and brother came home from labor service that evening. We decided to go to my mother's brother's house in her hometown, Sotome, Nishi Sonogi-gun. We waited for daybreak. Her hometown was eight kilometers from our house in Inasa.

My oldest sister carried our burnt brother on her back. On the way she frequently asked, "Are you still alive?" "Are you still alive?" She only started walking again when she knew he was breathing.

When we came to Ohashi Bridge over the Urakami River, we saw a crowd of people who looked like seals. They were completely black with soot. Most of them were mumbling something about water. They walked right into the river and were washed away.

My brother was thirsty and kept weakly gasping, "Water, water." We had heard that if we gave him water he would die. We managed to

Hiding my A-bomb exposure from my husband, my honeymoon was agony.

Yuriyo Hama
Born October 1935. Exposed to the atomic bombing at home in Inasa-machi, two kilometers from the hypocenter. She was nine years old. After losing her mother to the atomic bombing, she and her older siblings had to make a living by themselves. After graduation from junior high school she worked for a mandarin orange canning plant but was forced to quit by severe anemia. Married at 22. Was often confined to bed due to poor health, but delivered a healthy girl. Seventy-nine years old. Resides in Kinkai Ohira-machi, Nagasaki City.

I picked up my mother's ashes and put them in a broken bowl.

Yuriyo Hama was the fourth of seven children, three boys and four girls. Her eldest sister was 15, her eldest brother was 13, and she was nine at the time of the bombing. Her father had been sent to Saipan; her mother and the children lived in Inasa-machi. Her eldest sister and brother commuted to the Mitsubishi Shipyard for labor service.

Because my mother was physically weak, she always called me to her side and made me help her take care of things. She always said, "Girls must be modest."

August 9, 1945, 11:02 am. A yellow alert had cleared, and the whole City was silent, quiet enough to be eerie.

That morning we had received some rations from the neighborhood association. Each family got two handfuls of adzuki beans. My mother put a pot on the kitchen stove and was cooking sweet bean soup using

Nagasaki August 9, 1945

I get even slightly sick I get a stinging pain near my stomach. I feel fear, wondering if I've finally come down with some terrible disease. More than burns and injuries, I think the primary suffering of survivors is our anxiety, the lack of normal peace of mind. I have lived with this anxiety for 70 years.

Even my wife asked me why I haven't talked about my exposure to the atomic bombing all through these years. The fact is, I didn't want to remember. But soon after my daughter entered high school, she said, "We have to make a collection of essays to pass on the atomic bombing. Please tell me your story." I turned her down at first, but in the end, I decided to tell her.

To tell the truth, I still would prefer not to remember.

saying, "I heard the city was totally destroyed by a new type of bomb. I was sure you were dead."

The Mitsubishi Electric factory was destroyed; no operations were possible. It remained closed for more than two years. When it reopened, Nobuharu returned to work and stayed until retirement.

I got married in 1953. My company often held parties in a certain chanpon restaurant. (Chanpon is a Nagasaki specialty, a bit like ramen.) In that restaurant a certain young woman lived and worked. The proprietress of the restaurant knew my uncle, and the two of them would talk about me marrying that young woman.

My future wife's mother said, "Even if he's poor, I want your husband to be healthy." I looked a bit pale, so they made me submit a certificate of health. My mother-in-law knew I was a survivor. According to my wife, when she had our first son, her mother came into the hospital and subtly counted our son's fingers and toes. Sure enough, she had been worried.

I was inside the factory and didn't breathe the "radioactive gas." I was convinced there was no reason for me to be affected. As far as I was concerned, the only aftereffect of the atomic bombing was the scar behind my ear where I had been cut by a glass fragment. However, a medical checkup I had when the factory reopened found that I had a stomach ulcer. Around that time, my health deteriorated. I frequently had diarrhea. I carried with me a medicine for intestinal disorders and took it often. My thyroid was weak, and whenever I got sick, my throat would swell up.

I am not willing to talk much about my anxiety. It is something you simply cannot understand if you were not exposed. It's so cruel. When

engine. It grew quiet, then flew back down in a fast dive. The engine came back on at a height where they could clearly see our boat. The machinegun began firing as the plane buzzed the surface of the water, then climbed high again.

We were under attack, so naturally, screaming and chaos filled the boat. Every one of us wondered why a boat stopped in the middle of a harbor with no oar should be the target of an enemy plane. Then, we discovered that the oar was attached to the boat by a string, so we could use the string to pull the oar back.

When I talk about it now, it's ridiculous, even funny, but there, on the border between life and death, we were completely out of our minds. I shrank myself as small as possible and concentrated on praying for safe passage to Ohato.

I will never forget the sound of that machinegun firing bullets into the water making a pyun pyun sound. Perhaps the gunner was upset or a beginner, but miraculously, no one was shot. We arrived safely in Ohato. From there, I took a long detour home to Kamikoshima.

On the way home I saw the area behind Ohato (now, the area around the Nagasaki Prefectural Government building). The entire area was a sea of fire. That fire burned continuously for three days and three nights. Then, heavy rain fell for a few days. In Kamikoshima we had normal heavy rain, but I heard some places had black rain.

When I returned home, I found all the window glass shattered, but other than that, the house was undamaged. My mother had died a few years earlier and my younger brother also had died from tuberculosis when he was small. Therefore, I lived with my father, who worked for a printing company.

I arrived home in the evening. My father, who was saved by a shelter, came home later that night. He was overjoyed to see me

There's no way to miss a white summer shirt, but nobody was shot. I still wonder why.

The enemy plane left but the municipal boat captain never came. I got irritated, but when I think about it now, what followed was like a cartoon.

At that time, beside the municipal boat, which was like a bus service, quite a few people bought and used tenmasen as their transport vehicles. A tenmasen was a boat rowed with a single oar in the back, like a sampan or gondola. Creak. Creak. Given the tension around us at that moment, the sampan appeared utterly foolish, but people worried about what had happened in Nagasaki were arriving by sampan.

When the passengers got out of the sampan, those of us on the pier started fighting to get on board. The boat was soon full, but there was no one to row it. One of us took the oar and started rowing based on his imagination of how to row a sampan.

When we got to the middle of the river the same enemy plane came back. Now we were in a panic. The sampan was just slightly bigger than a rowboat, and there was no place to hide.

"Hurry up! What are you doing, idiot?"

"Turn right!"

Everyone complained and blamed the rower, but he was a beginner and was completely upset. He seemed to hit his wrist on something. His watchband broke and the watch dropped into the water. He tried to grab the sinking watch. Thrusting himself forward, he fell into the water himself. We pulled him out of the water while chasing the enemy plane with our eyes. As we did that, the oar slipped off the oarlock. We were left with no choice but to float helplessly wherever the river would take us.

The enemy plane flew high into the sky. It seemed to turn off its

Nagasaki August 9, 1945

hair was scorched and frizzy, their skin hideously burned, and their clothes were in tatters.

Even though it was mid-summer, most people in the shelter were shivering and saying, "I'm cold."

The sights I saw when I left the factory to go home were too horrible to believe. Among the people rushing to escape faster than others was a person tottering unsteadily, looking exactly like a terribly burned ghost. A woman clung tightly to her dead baby, yelling in delirium. People like these were everywhere. I finally reached Inasa Bridge.

Probably because it was almost noon and so many households had been preparing lunch, fires quickly broke out here and there, spreading rapidly. The entire Urakami area was soon a sea of fire. Wooden homes were the first to go. Concrete buildings were blazing by evening.

I saw a streetcar with its whole top blown off. Its passengers lay dead, piled on top of one another and the now-open streetcar floor. Streetcar rails were raised and twisted like a roller coaster rail. Terribly burnt cows and horses lay toppled in the road.

I wanted to get home, but I thought it might be dangerous to cross Inasa Bridge. I decided to cross the river by municipal boat. I turned around and headed for a municipal boat pier thinking I could get a ride to Ohato Warf.

At the pier they said they couldn't launch the boat because the captain had run away. While we were speaking, an enemy plane appeared and fired its machine gun fiercely in our direction.

We all ran this way and that to escape from this unexpected strafing. Some hid under the pier. Others threw themselves on the floor.

middle fingers and threw myself to the ground. We had been drilled to do this to protect our eyes and ears. As we worked, a citizen soldier would suddenly shout, "Down!!" And we would have to get into that posture as quickly as possible. Because of this training, I was able to take quick action.

Just as I got into the posture, window glass from the high factory ceiling came crashing down with a roar. I wore a combat cap and work uniform, so my head and body were protected. Still, a sharp glass fragment struck the back of my right ear. I felt warm blood rolling into my face. What if the glass fragment had been slightly to the left. It might have struck my carotid artery. I shudder to think of it. I still have the scar from that cut.

When Nobuharu raised his head, he saw the roof had been totally blown off by the blast. The factory building had been reduced to an iron frame. He was looking outside as dust and dirt from the factory billowed high into the sky.

The opposite side of the factory was a woodshop for female workers. A volunteer corps from Kumamoto Girls School had come for training in making searchlights. Because their building was wooden, many workers were killed.

I saw my co-workers at the factory running toward the shelter behind the factory. We called it a shelter, but it was just a hole scooped out of the rocky slope of the mountain. It had been used as a test site for large turbine generators. Over 1200 factory workers rushed there all at once.

Many who had been working in the factory were bleeding, like me, due to injuries from glass shards or other objects hurled by the blast. Those who had been working outside were in worse condition. Their

Nagasaki August 9, 1945

I broke my long silence because my daughter said, "We have to make a book about the A-bomb experience."

Nobuharu Takahira
Born in December 1928. Exposed to the atomic bombing at the Mitsubishi Electric factory near Nagasaki Port, 3 kilometers from the hypocenter. He was 16. His health deteriorated after exposure, and he has lived with great anxiety. He was assigned to Mitsubishi Electric for labor service and worked there until retirement. Talked about his A-bomb experience for the first time because his daughter said, "We have to make a collection of essays to preserve the A-bomb experience." Eighty-six years old; resides in Sakai, Nagasaki City.

Anxiety was the deeper pain.

Nobuharu Takahira was a second year student at Nita Post-Elementary School. He was going to graduate in four months. His job was to connect rotating parts to fixed parts in ship motors at a Mitsubishi Electric factory near Nagasaki Port. This was his official "labor service".

It was a perfectly clear day. Nobuharu heard the buzzing B-29 bombers and looked toward the sky from a factory window, but he didn't see anything.

While looking at the window, I noticed the clock over the entrance to the factory and was just looking to see what time it was. In that instant a pure white flash came in horizontally through the window. As soon as I turned my face toward the flash, I heard a tremendous booooom!

I pressed my ears with my thumbs and my eyes with my index and

I write the names of those who passed away during the previous year into the "Register of A-bomb Victims" which is placed in the symbolic coffin each year on "Nagasaki Day" (August 9). I have been doing this since 2006 at the request of Nagasaki City.

When I began writing these lists I visited my brother (5th son) in the hospital where he was waiting for a heart operation. I told him what I was doing, and he encouraged me. "That's an important task so do your best."

Soon after that conversation, the hospital hurried to conduct his operation, but he died two weeks later. I never thought I would be writing my own brother's name on that list the first year I started the job.

From the day I received that writing request to this day, I never fail to make myself visit the Atomic Bomb Museum a few days before I start writing. Looking at the exhibits I think about the victims. I pray sincerely saying, "Please let me hold the brush with my desire for peace and a prayer for the peaceful repose of the souls."

I write the names, age at death and date of death for each of the departed, and what I write will be preserved forever. Naturally, I am absolutely determined to write as carefully as I can.

Every year on August 9 when the list is placed safely in the coffin, I feel a relief that comes from the bottom of my heart.

we were four kilometers from the hypocenter. But our area was actually behind a small hill. Many of the houses were shielded by that hill, which is why so many were undamaged. Other neighborhoods also four kilometers away were badly damaged because the blast hit them directly.

Later, my brother the firefighter who was doing rescue work said, "We headed for the Urakami District to help. Streetcar cables were hanging down. Houses, schools and factory buildings were collapsed or burning. Water pipes were broken so we couldn't fight the fire or do much of anything." That brother (3rd son) died of lung cancer. The brother who had been with me (5th son) died of heart disease. It's strange that my parents, my sisters and I have apparently had no aftereffects from the atomic bombing.

Because Masahiro's brothers died, his father suggested that he get an Atomic Bomb Survivor Health Book. He applied in his mid-twenties. To get the health book he needed two people to testify that he had been in the bombing. It had been nearly 20 years, and the neighbors in his old neighborhood had moved away. No one was left who knew Masahiro as a child. He had hard time finding people to testify for him, but he succeeded eventually.

Masahiro entered night school to get his high school graduation equivalent and worked at City Hall during the day. He stayed at City Hall after graduating. Masahiro loved calligraphy. He had never studied it formally at schools, but he was often assigned to write certificates because his handwriting was so beautiful. After retiring he got requests from local associations to write certificates of commendation and from schools to write diplomas.

His wife is from Saikai City and not a survivor. Still, no one on her side of the family opposed marriage with a survivor.

After a few days a rumor flew around town. "The occupation army is landing. Women and children will be massacred." People in my neighborhood fled to their relatives' homes. My family decided to evacuate to Nishi Arie-cho (now, Minami Shimabara City) where some distant relatives of my mother lived.

Nagasaki station was burnt out and no trains were running so six of my family members departed toward evening of the 14th. We walked all the night and finally arrived at Isahaya where trains would available at dawn on the 15th.

We were allowed to rest in a temple nearby. The temple was overflowing with the people escaping. I will never forget how delicious the rice ball I was given was.

I heard the Emperor's announcement at that temple.

We went from Isahaya to Nishi Arie by train.

My mother's relatives were the main branch of our family tree and, therefore, had a large farm house. I played with my sisters in their huge yard.

They had already accepted many families came from elsewhere, so they said, "There's no place for you." We stayed there one night and returned to our home in Nagasaki. I remember my father being in a very bad mood in the train going home.

The city right after the bombing was a ruin. It was full of debris with smoke still rising from the smoldering remains. I saw corpses charred so badly even the gender was unrecognizable. One person's arm was torn off but barely held onto the body by skin. I saw a mother wandering in daze holding her dead baby. Some people were struggling to stuff their internal organs back into their torsos. Later I heard that people like the ones I saw were all over the city. Many simply fell to the ground moaning, "Water, I need water."

At first I thought we had less damage in Nishi Koshima just because

Nagasaki August 9, 1945

He was injured at his work place (Nagasaki Customs) by glass shards blown through the air by the blast.

When night fell, Masahiro, his parents and siblings went home. Their house was not even tilted. No roof tiles were blown away. It was fine.

His third oldest brother, who worked at a fire station two kilometers from the hypocenter, had been blown through the air in the station, but was not seriously injured. He immediately went out to do rescue work in the Urakami area. He received "Permission for Confirmation of Family Safety" from his chief that night and went home. He confirmed his family was safe. Greatly relieved, he went back to join the rescue work.

My brother and his team were helping to dispose of the vast number of corpses that littered the area. I personally remember that a site near my house where the Kannai Market had been before the bombing was used for cremation. Corpses were lined up there waiting their turn. Most came in almost naked. While they were waiting, the bodies were covered by summer kimono or given something to wear. People felt sorry to see them just lying there naked.

Workers brought pillars and beams from fallen houses and lay them in a cross-pair pattern like building a campfire. They laid the bodies on the pile of wood and kept them burning night and day. I still can't forget the light from those flames and the continual stench of burning bodies.

They cremated many bodies at once, so relatives would stand in rows around the fire waiting for the flames to die down. They didn't really know whose ashes were whose, but they all put some in their own boxes and took them home.

of disease in 1941. Masahiro was seven years old and a second grader at Sako Elementary School. He, his sixth-grade brother and younger sisters (five and two) were always together, usually playing happily.

That day my mother went out early to help our neighbors dig a shelter, a part of their "labor service". I was with my three siblings at home because an air-raid warning had sounded. After a while the warning cleared, so we talked for a while about what to do and decided to go find our mother. We headed for the place we thought she was working.

The shelter was being dug at a site about 200 meters from our house. The digging was done by women because the men had all gone off to military service. They used a claw hoe to loosen the earth, stuffed it into bamboo baskets, and carried the baskets outside. We had some time before lunch, so I was in an empty lot nearby catching dragonflies for my sisters.

Suddenly, a flash like a bolt of lightning filled the sky. We were terrified and ran into the shelter where our mother was. We heard nothing.

Someone shouted, "It's a bomb!"

Fortunately, none of us was injured, but injured people soon began coming into the shelter. Everyone was saying, "Nagasaki is gone."

When I went out. I saw the Nagasaki Prefectural Government Building burning and a black cloud hanging over the front of the station.

Someone said, ""It's too dangerous to go out now. You better stay here a while." So I stayed there with my mother and my siblings until evening. Some went home, worried about their houses.

My father came to the shelter that evening. He had a white curtain wound around his head like a turban; it was bright red with blood.

Nagasaki August 9, 1945

Enter the names of atomic bomb victims into the Register with a prayer.

Masahiro Tanigawa
Born December 1937. Exposed to the atomic bombing near his house in Nishi Koshima, four kilometers from the hypocenter when he was seven. Worked for Nagasaki City Hall while studying at a high school at night. After graduation, worked at City Hall, often called on to write certificates and other documents requiring especially nice penmanship. After retiring, began writing diplomas for schools. Still enters into the Register of A-bomb Victims the names of those who died during the previous year. The Register is placed in a symbolic coffin each year on the A-bomb memorial day. Seventy-seven years old; resides in Hayama, Nagasaki City.

While catching dragonflies for my sisters

Masahiro Tanigawa was the seventh of nine siblings (five older brothers, 1 older sister and two younger sisters.) His mother had four children with a previous husband, remarried and had five children with Masahiro's father, who worked for customs in Nagasaki.

Nishi Koshima, where the Tanigawa family lived, was the origin in Japan of Western medical science. As of 1855, it had the first medical school in Japan teaching Western medicine, with the first teacher from the Netherlands coming in 1857.

Masahiro's oldest brother was serving in the military; his second oldest brother was killed in combat. His third oldest brother worked as a firefighter in Nagasaki. His fourth oldest brother died

his exposure when we got married. There was a time when rumor had it that A-bomb survivors deliver deformed babies. Since my sisters had healthy babies, I didn't worry when I was pregnant. My children and grandchildren are all fine.

My father, my oldest and second oldest sisters died of heart disease. My mother died of liver and pancreatic cancers. My youngest sister died of uterine and colorectal cancers. My brother who developed so many diseases and was told that he wouldn't live until 10 is doing well. My younger sister and I had no major illnesses and are healthy today.

We must never allow our children, grandchildren or any of the generations to come suffer the pain that the atomic bomb survivors experienced.

Nagasaki August 9, 1945

During this time of severe shortages, Yasuko's father managed to find a paper carp banner to celebrate Boy's Day in May for Hatsuo. He put it up in front of the house. The colorful banner streaming in the wind was a great source of pride for Hatsuo's sisters, even though they were girls. In addition, for the New Year holiday, her parents made new dresses for all five sisters. They bought battledores and shuttlecocks for a game we played on New Year's Day. The ones they got were almost the same size and pattern. This was to avoid fighting. The girls compared what they received saying, "Mine is this or that, how about yours?"

My brother Hatsuo started to walk holding onto furniture at about one. But after he walked 2 or 3 steps, he would fall heavily on his seat. I remember thinking that was strange. He developed big boils on both sides of his belly. They swelled up big and red. Soon they broke and discharged pus. He screamed loud and long because of the pain. I felt so sorry to see such big boils on such a small body.

He was taken to a hospital where the doctor opened his boils. After cleaning out the pus, they filled them with gauze but the openings of the wounds were like gaping holes. They looked very painful.

The doctor said, "He won't live to be 10 years old." Before long, his boils were completely healed, but his backbone remained bent due to the aftereffects. He also developed myocardial infarction, cerebral infarction and other illnesses one after another. I have often thought this could have been due to in-utero exposure.

After graduating from school I took various jobs. My last job was to make Chinese confections. I worked there until I was 68.

My husband is also an A-bomb survivor, but I didn't worry about

took us to the site but the fire had already gone out. It was just coals and ash.

There was a beautiful beach right behind our shed, and when it got dark and the other people left, our oldest sister took us to dig for shellfish. The villagers had already dug the shellfish mercilessly so there were almost none left. But our younger sisters were happy playing with sand and digging small shells. I also felt some brief enjoyment. We found some beautiful empty shells and took them home to play with.

Meanwhile, we got a brother in October. People around us were still thinking exposure to the atomic bombing was like a contagious disease. My mother delivered our brother by herself in the shed with no help from any midwife or nurse.

My sisters who were 12 and 10 helped my mother's delivery by boiling hot water and collecting cloth rags according to her directions. Our brother was given the name Hatsuo because he was the first boy in our family. We five sisters took every opportunity to surround him, touch him, and rub him. Even though our mother scolded us, we couldn't stay away from him.

The following year Yasuko's father built a shack in the city so the family went back to Nagasaki. Nagasaki in May, eight months after the atomic bombing, was still a burnt plain.

I entered Nishizaka Elementary School in 1946. It was called a school but it was a hastily constructed wooden building with few classrooms and not enough of anything. First and second graders shared a room, one in the morning, the other in the afternoon. Sometimes we were taught while sitting on the stone steps outside.

parents or relatives came to Nagasaki to take them home. It seemed to me they were taken on board without sufficient treatment. Their wounds were open burns festering and drawing swarms of flies.

A large number were already dead. I'm sure the parents at least wanted to have their loved one buried on the home island. Corpses were wrapped in blankets and laid on stretchers. I felt pity for them to some extent, but I couldn't bear that horrible smell. All I wanted was to get out of that boat as soon as possible.

We finally arrived at my father's brother's house, but we were treated badly because we were "exposed to the atomic bombing." My father's brother's family lived in a rural area far from Nagasaki City. No one had been exposed and no one understood our suffering. They hated my family because they thought the atomic bomb was contagious. They worried about what the other villagers might think. Not only did they refuse to let us into their house, they didn't let us into the empty annex either. We were given a shed that was filled with farm equipment and fertilizer. We borrowed some fields around the shed and planted vegetables on our own to have something to eat.

Our father had a job in Nagasaki and soon went back to work. Once we were an all-female household, the discrimination went from bad to terrible.

The Dondo festival was the finale of the New Year's celebration. This big event in the village featured the burning of ornaments displayed during the New Year holidays. Feeling the excitement, my younger sisters and I were eager to go out. They told us "Don't leave the shed while village people are at the festival."

I begged my mother saying I wanted to go to the festival. She looked sad and said, "We owe them our lives so let's forget about it."

My oldest sister had gone several times to see what was going on at the festival and finally confirmed that all the villagers were gone. She

living hell.

Yasuko's grandmother's house was further up the hill from Yasuko's home. Fortunately that house was between a road and a cliff so the fire didn't get it. Since her grandmother's house had escaped the fire, they moved in there after her father came back. Twenty relatives from four families who had lived in Nagasaki sought shelter there and lived under one roof for some time.

We should never allow our descendants to suffer the agony of an atomic bombing.

I learned the war had ended from the Emperor's announcement of Japan's surrender, which was broadcast on August 15th, but I couldn't understand the meaning of "the end of the war". Overall, it seemed the adults were feeling relief that the B-29s would not be coming anymore.

I believe it was the day after the end of the war. I had not uttered a scream or cry at the time of the atomic bombing, but when a thunderclap sounded even though it wasn't raining, I was so scared I jumped up and screamed. The adults around me also thought an enemy plane had come. My father went so far as to clasp his youngest daughter to his side and rush out of the house.

At the end of August my whole family boarded a ship from the port at Ohato to go to my father's brother's house. Today, we can go there in an hour by car, but in those days there was no road. We had to go by ferry, and there was no direct ferry. We changed boats several times. The boats got smaller and smaller until the last one, a rowboat, landed with only my family on board.

There were many injured victims on the bigger boats. During the war many students were mobilized from far away islands to Nagasaki City. Those students were exposed to the atomic bombing, and their

Nagasaki August 9, 1945

People in the shelter were grumbling and groaning. "The house is burning! My house is burning!" When the fire spread to Nishizaka Elementary School, a heavy sigh echoed through the shelter.

Eventually, even our house on top of the mountain was enveloped in flames. We watched our house burn from a field in front of the shelter. The fire burned bright red making the night as bright as day. We could do nothing but watch in a daze.

Because their house was burned, Yasuko and her family stayed in the shelter for some time. The shelter was filled with people, leaving no space to stretch out. Yasuko and her older sisters leaned on their mother, being careful not to push on her belly. Her younger sisters rested on their mother's lap.

In the evening when it got cool, some people left the shelter, but being afraid a B-29 might come at any moment, they laid down in a field or under a tree just to stretch their bodies. It was the height of summer and eggplants, tomatoes and sweet potatoes grew in the fields. Because they had no way to cook anything, they ate the eggplants, tomatoes and sweet potatoes raw. Yasuko looks back at that time saying, "It's horrifying that we ate food so covered by radiation."

It took their father two days to find them. He had been working at the ordnance factory, and they were sure he was dead. They were suffering in grief when, to their surprise, he somehow managed to get back to them despite a severe leg injury.

Their father told them what he had seen on his way back. People roaming around begging for water. People washed alive down the Urakami River. A baby still sucking at the breast of his dead mother. People whose skin was hideously burned and in tatters, even their gender unrecognizable, groaning, "Hot! I'm so hot!" He described a

due to the extreme horror. We didn't even have the ability to cry.

My oldest sister and other older children who saw the completely transformed landscape around us led us toward the shelter on top of the mountain where my mother and neighbors were working. The road was blocked by debris from fallen buildings. We could hardly walk.

On the way, we saw a man was stirring the water in a reservoir with a bamboo stick, crying.

I asked him, "What are you doing?"

He said, "My son and I were working in the field and now he's gone."

I learned later that the child had been thrown into the reservoir and plunged to the bottom.

Fighting our way around the debris, we finally arrived at the shelter after almost an hour, though it usually took about 10 minutes. By the time we arrived, our mother was nowhere to be seen. Later we learned that, despite her big belly holding an unborn baby, she and some others had been carrying large logs with which to support the ceiling of the shelter to keep it from falling down. We found her climbing the stone steps from the vacant lot next to the school. She said she had been blown all the way down to the waterway by the blast. However, she had no serious injury and did not lose the baby. As soon as my younger sisters saw our mother, they clung to her and, for the first time since the bomb exploded, started crying.

Because of Nagasaki's hills and valleys, we couldn't see the area around the hypocenter. We didn't know what had happened.

That evening, black smoke rose up from the area near Nagasaki Station. The flame sped fiercely up the slope. The remaining houses started burning one after another. By nightfall, the whole area was a sea of fire.

Nagasaki August 9, 1945

At first when an air-raid warning sounded, the whole family put on air-raid hoods. I carried a backpack stuffed with Buddhist memorial tablets. My older sisters each took one of the younger sisters, and we all fled to the shelter. Later, we stopped going to the shelter because my mother was pregnant. She could barely get to the top of the mountain, and we were afraid that we would burn to death before we got to the shelter. We decided, "If we're going to die, we'll all die together!" After that, we never took refuge in the shelter at night. We stayed at home huddling around our mother.

On August 9th my mother went out early in the morning with our neighbors to work on the shelter on the top of the mountain. All the adults from every house were mobilized to work on the shelter, and I believe only about ten children were left at home.

That morning an air-raid warning sounded. My oldest sister took us to the shelter, but the warning changed to a yellow alert so we left the shelter and went home. I was playing housewife in an empty lot in front of my home with other neighborhood children.

After 11:00 am, all of a sudden everything turned pure white in front of my eyes, then turned pitch black. When I thought about it later, I realized that the flash from the atomic bomb was so intense I couldn't see anything at all for a while.

As I was gradually able to see the scene around me, everything had changed. Houses had collapsed. Roof tiles had blown away. Sliding paper doors, window frames and even pickle jars that had been in a kitchen were scattered outside.

Gradually I realized that I, too, had been blown some distance by the blast. My second oldest sister was bleeding. It looked like something blowing through the air had hit her head. Maybe she was too stunned, but she didn't even cry out in pain. None of the children I had been playing with was crying. No one was able to make a sound

Discriminated against because "the atomic bomb is contagious"

Yasuko Nakao
Born in July 1939. Exposed to the atomic bombing while playing with children in her neighborhood near Nishizaka Elementary School, 1.8 kilometers from the hypocenter. After living in her grandmother's house, then her father's brother's house, she lived in a shack her father built in Nagasaki. Entered Nishizaka Elementary School. Married a survivor and worked until 68, remains healthy at seventy-five and resides in Fukahori-machi, Nagasaki City.

Yasuko Nakao was the third of five girls. Her family of seven included both parents and sisters 12, 10, 4 and 3 years old. They lived near Nishizaka Elementary School. The sisters were always together, lively and happy with each other.

Their house next to Nishizaka Elementary School was surrounded by fields at the foot of a mountain. There was a bomb shelter near the top of the mountain; they had to climb steep stone steps beside the school to get up to it. Her father worked for an ordnance factory and was seldom home.

Because of extreme terror, we couldn't make a sound.

In those days, a yellow alert would sound, then quickly become an air-raid warning. Air raids came in the middle of the night. B29s flew over in formation and sprinkled red-hot incendiary bombs. As soon as an incendiary bomb hit, the ground instantly burst into flame.

my mouth always felt bad. These symptoms continued for some time even after I came back to Nagasaki City. I got high blood pressure early and was unable to go without medicine.

However, turning 20, I have been completely normal. When I got married my exposure was never a problem.

say, "When the maggots move, it hurts a lot."

Another person was doing nothing but vomiting blood into a washbowl. Others had lost their hair to the flash. I couldn't tell if they were male or female. And the terrible stench was making me sick. Mixed with that burned odor was the smell of dead bodies. The smell of a dead body is peculiar, indescribable, and horrible. And that smell was everywhere the rest of that year.

After six months, Tsugiya and his sisters left Minami Shimabara and went back to Nagasaki. His brother contracted spinal caries after the wound on his back became infected. His mother stayed in the hospital all day to care for his brother. Tsugiya visited the hospital every day to deliver meals to his mother.

My brother also had a burn on his left arm, which got infected and was slow to heal. He got spinal caries, which deformed his backbone. However, his condition did not continue to degenerate, and he is still alive and well.

My three sisters exposed to the atomic bombing in Hiroshima have been in poor health. They have never been diagnosed with any specific illnesses, so they don't know what is wrong, but they are always in poor physical condition. They spend more days in bed as they get older. I believe their health is deteriorating slowly but steadily.

I graduated from the Faculty of Education at Nagasaki University. I became a teacher at Doi-no-kubi Elementary School in Nagasaki City in April 1957 and taught for seven years. I then worked many years for the Nagasaki Peace Hall. I am now retired and in good shape.

I suffered the effects of the atomic bombing the whole time I lived in Minami Shimabara. I was always tired and could hardly get up. I frequently had to lie down quickly. I was bleeding from my gums, and

Nagasaki August 9, 1945

myself. Now, we had a cheerful, lively family, with my father, mother and grandma all talking in loud voices rejoicing at being safe and with each other again.

In Hiroshima, the whole family had been trapped under the house. Fortunately, my father had been at home getting ready to go to work. He helped the others one by one, pulling them out from under the collapsed house.

My sisters were just scratched but my younger brother suffered a serious injury when a beam fell on his back. My parents, sisters and brother were exposed to the bombing in Hiroshima; my grandma and I were in Nagasaki. And yet, we had suffered little damage and were alive. We all celebrated our good fortune.

Later on Tsugiya and his three sisters evacuated to Futsu-cho in Minami Shimabara, his father's hometown. They rode the train just after service was restored. His mother remained at his grandmother's house with his injured brother. His father took Tsugiya and his sisters to his parents' house and left them there, returning to his work place in Hiroshima.

From the window of the train I saw the burnt bodies of people who had been working on their farms. They were still lying there abandoned, though almost two weeks had passed since the atomic bombing. I noticed white foam around the mouth of a charred body. Later I realized that foam must have been maggots.

Inside the train was also gruesome. In the hottest days of summer, burned arms and legs soon rotted, attracting swarms of flies. The flies just kept coming, even though people did their best to chase them away. One person's wound was just covered with white maggots. It seemed his mother was picking them out with chopsticks. I heard him

was nothing we could do, so we just went home. The following day we still could do nothing but worry if we stayed at home waiting, so we went back to the ruins of the station. This time, we saw a streetcar all burned and smoldering.

A person in a shirt dyed with blood appeared to be wandering in a daze. A woman carrying a child on her back was asking everyone if her family was safe. Some people were just standing vacantly in front of collapsed houses. They had probably come from the countryside to find their relatives. The scene through the whole city was gruesome.

People with "Relief" armbands carried corpses, and fire brigade members were finding scraps of wood to burn the corpses. Surrounding them were people standing in shock, watching the flames consume their loved ones. They had no more tears to shed because they had already cried their last teardrops.

Tsugiya's grandmother fell ill on August 13th. They gave up going back to the station. The following afternoon, on the 14th, his parents arrived from Hiroshima bringing his brother and three sisters, all in the condition they were left in by the atomic bombing.

They had departed from Miyajima, located west of Hiroshima, but because of the bombing the trains were in turmoil. It took four days to get to Michino-o station. From there, Tsugiya's father carried his injured brother on his back. They walked all the way through the burnt plain of Nagasaki.

Rather than joy, I first felt tremendous surprise. My parents and siblings were standing in front of me. My grandma was so happy she cooked all the rice she had saved and all the potatoes. I still remember that day whenever I eat a potato.

The dining table had been so quiet with just my grandma and

Mountain, a large iron ball in that tower would slide to the bottom. If not for Boom Mountain, those of us at Gourd River would have been directly exposed to the flash and blast. We'd have been blown away.

I heard that a similar bomb had fallen on Hiroshima a few days earlier, and I immediately worried about my parents and siblings. When we heard the rumor that "Hiroshima was completely destroyed," I couldn't sit still, I was so full of anxiety. My grandma and I decided to go to Nagasaki Station. Because they had lived in Nagasaki until quite recently, we thought they would surely come to Nagasaki to stay with grandma.

The houses in Hinode-machi were spared, thanks to Boom Mountain, so many relatives of neighborhood residents came looking for help.

We headed for Nagasaki Station following the streetcar tracks. From Hinode-machi, we passed Ishibashi streetcar stop. As we went toward Dejima and Ohato, the damage to houses became more obvious. Some buildings were blown away leaving no trace of their original form. After a while, we couldn't even tell where we were walking. Debris was everywhere; we couldn't see the road.

A cart lay on its side. The horse that had been pulling it had burned to death. Corpses were lying all around us.

When we arrived at what we thought was Nagasaki Station, we were stunned. The station building was gone, completely burned out, with no trains in sight. Almost everything around the station was burned. The steel skeletons of buildings were left standing but twisted like taffy.

The railway was not going to be fixed any time soon. We learned that the trains were stopped at Michino-o, two stations away. There

the river. The Gourd River was shallow, with water only up to our knees. When we put our net below the bank and stirred up the water, the river shrimp came into the net. We were having great fun.

We were completely concentrating on our enjoyable task when suddenly, there was a flash like a tremendous bolt of lightning. We rushed into the shelter in a panic and were there by the time we heard the tremendous boooommm!

So much dirt fell from the ceiling of the shelter that I was buried. We called it a shelter, but it was actually just a tunnel dug by neighborhood volunteers. It always looked like it could collapse any time.

I couldn't move because of fear and the dirt. I stayed still for a long time. The mothers of the boys I was with came looking for us. They dug us out.

Then we went outside and looked around for the first time. It was probably an hour after I had been buried in the shelter. The summer sky was so dark it could have been night. And fires were springing up here and there and spreading quickly.

Tsugiya's grandmother came to the shelter looking for him, and they went home together. On the way, they walked through roof tiles that had fallen from the houses. Broken glass was everywhere. Even furniture was scattered around on the road.

We have many mountains in Nagasaki. Because Hinode-machi was sheltered behind Boom Mountain, our house remained standing. We call it Boom Mountain because a cannon at the summit always boomed to let us know it was noon.

A steel tower on Mt. Nabe Kanmuri stood facing Boom Mountain a few kilometers away. Whenever the boom came from Boom

Nagasaki August 9, 1945

I was sent to a temple in Saijo, Hiba-gun, a rural part of Hiroshima Prefecture. I was separated from my parents. My first experience of life without my family was terribly lonely. In addition, we never had enough food so I was always hungry.

A typical meal was rice gruel with a few mountain vegetables like Japanese butterbur, bracken and royal fern fiddleheads picked in mountains. But after eating, I was still hungry. I often tore the skin off a stick of knotweed and nibbled it's sour inner stem.

I also remember one sunny day smashing lice crawling in lines along the seams of my shirt with the tip of my fingernail.

Our letters to parents were censored by the teachers. We were told not to complain or even say, "I miss my house," because our parents would worry about us.

All I had to look forward to was gifts sent occasionally by my parents. It was usually dry bread, which I shared with friends who didn't get gifts from home.

Tsugiya's grandmother lived in Nagasaki and sent a letter asking his parents to "send me one of my grandchildren. I'm lonely." His parents decided to send Tsugiya because he was away from home anyway. Tsugiya's two months of "group evacuation" would end and become "relative evacuation." He went off to live in Nagasaki.

August 9, 1945 began with a clear, sunny morning. I was playing in a river near a shelter dug by people in my neighborhood. It was just upstream of Shiinoki River. Because the river suddenly widened at that spot, it was called Gourd River. I was catching river shrimp with two boys in my neighborhood.

An air-raid warning that morning had kept me waiting impatiently at home. When the warning was cleared, we met up and headed for

My parents, younger brother and three younger sisters were exposed in Hiroshima; my grandmother and I were exposed three days later in Nagasaki.

Tsugiya Umebayashi
Born in December 1934. Exposed to the atomic bombing at 11 while playing in a river in Hinode-machi, 4.5 kilometers from the Nagasaki hypocenter. Parents and siblings exposed in Hiroshima. After graduation from Faculty of Education, Nagasaki University, taught at Doi-no-kubi Elementary School for 7 years. Retired from work and in good shape. Eighty years old, resides in Shiinoki-machi, Nagasaki City.

The smell of dead bodies everywhere

Tsugiya Umebayashi was a 4th grader at Hiroshima Municipal Kan-on Elementary School. He lived in Kan-on Shin-machi, several kilometers from the hypocenter in Hiroshima in 1944. His father, who previously worked at Mitsubishi Heavy Industries Nagasaki Shipyard, was transferred to Hiroshima and moved his family there.

Tsugiya was the third son and 10 years old. He had three sisters, 8, 7, and less than a year. He also had a 4-year-old brother.

When air raids on the mainland intensified, group evacuations of schoolchildren began. Those who had relatives in the countryside were sent to "relative evacuations." Those who didn't were sent to "group evacuations" with groups of students.

Nagasaki August 9, 1945

the Mitsubishi Ordnance Plant at Dozaki. On the day of the bombing he entered the City from Dozaki and was disposing of corpses. Thus, he was an "entry survivor".

At one point, he told me, "The stench was so bad I couldn't do the disposal work without drinking some alcohol." According to him, a massive amount of expensive whisky and brandy were hidden by the military in his plant.

My husband constantly complained that his body was itching. I always suspected it was due to radiation. He passed away in 2002.

My father, a fire brigade member who went near the hypocenter many times for relief activities, died of gallbladder cancer. My youngest brother is always in and out of the hospital because of colorectal and gastric cancer. My youngest sister, the one who took such good care of me, is suffering from irregular pulse, hypertrophy of the heart and angina.

I obtained official recognition of my atomic bomb disease when I fell ill in 2006. I had a high fever of unknown cause for about a week. I was hospitalized with heart failure in the summer of 2014. The examination revealed that I had a valvular disease of the heart. Because of my age, the doctors are studying whether or not I should have an operation.

I was hospitalized with irregular pulse in 2011. Right before leaving the hospital, I was found to have colorectal cancer. Six months later, I had an operation for skin cancer. A body exposed to radiation is always standing next to death. I have made it for 70 years despite having been given up for lost, but my battle with radiation continues.

Less than an hour after I arrived at the first-aid station, we were informed that a US hospital ship had arrived at the port with a load of medical supplies. They decided to start by treating me and others who just arrived.

In my case, treatment meant blood transfusions. Every day I received more blood and grew stronger. I was soon on the path to recovery. I went home on the 45th day. When they saw me come walking home, my parents and all my family members were amazed. They gave me a big, warm welcome.

From the time we first took refuge in the shelter, my hair had been falling off. Soon I was bald. Even after I returned home, my hair kept falling out mercilessly. It grew, but was like baby hair. I was struck with grief whenever I saw my head. I couldn't go out in public.

I had wanted to be an elementary school teacher. I remember talking with a classmate in my neighborhood saying, "We'll be teachers together." When I heard that she became a teacher, I knew I was supposed to be glad for her, but the truth is, I was very sad.

Ryoko recuperated at home for a year. When she was able, she was hired as a nurse's assistant at a relative's clinic. Two years later, she got a job at the post office. After working two years for the post office, in 1951, she got married. The marriage was arranged by her mother's friend. Ryoko was 23 years old.

Maybe this was only around me, but it seemed that people I knew did not consider the effects of radiation much of a problem. Therefore, I had not spoken about my exposure to my husband and had not asked him about his. I learned only later that my husband was also an A-bomb survivor. He had been working in the torpedo test facility of

appeared, the patient would die.

Ryoko became so weak she couldn't even drink water. Her family heard that Shin-kozen Elementary School had become a first-aid station where a doctor from the University Hospital was treating survivors. They decided to take Ryoko there. Even so, everyone believed there was no hope for Ryoko. Even the local doctor had told them to give up.

I, too, thought, "I guess I'll never come home." I gave the dolls I had treasured since I was small, along with some beautiful colored papers I had saved, to my sisters and brothers saying, "Please share these when I die."

The day I left for the first-aid station I was on a wooden door. As I lay there, I looked carefully around my house thinking this would be the last time I would see it.

I was the first child. I had three younger sisters and two younger brothers. When my siblings sent me off, they were all crying. I have a dim memory of neighbors seeing me off along the road.

Although it was called a first-aid station, it was just an elementary school. There was nothing like a bed, just straw mats spread out on the floor. My family had brought a futon. They laid it out and laid me on it.

I was assigned to a classroom on the second floor and was put by a window. At one point I happened to look outside and saw a truck parked in front of the school. Dead bodies were being carried out on doors and loaded onto the truck. There was a pile of half-naked corpses on the bed of the truck. When they moved a body that had just been put onto the truck, I saw its head, more like a skull, roll down away from the body. I was terrified, thinking that was going to happen to me.

but some was left deep in my body, where it remained a long time. Years later, the remaining pieces would start to hurt.

Each time I felt pain, I had to go to the hospital and have a doctor cut my healed wounds to pick out another piece. He was getting pieces that were small, like grains of rice. I had about seven such pieces removed, but I still have tingling and scraping feelings around my knee, even after 70 years.

The most difficult thing was not being able to lie on my back. In fact, I had to keep both of my arms elevated all the time or blood gushed from my elbows. We piled futon under my left side, which had fewer wounds, and I slept leaning over the pile of futon with my arms over my head.

My sister spoon-fed me rice gruel and water. She wiped the blood and sweat from my face and body, constantly changing the water in the washbowl. She was a loving nurse, but those were days of hell to me.

There was no medicine, of course. I only got Mercurochrome for my wounds. When the gashes on my elbows closed and made scabs, my elbows wouldn't bend. To keep that from happening, the doctor forced my elbows to bend. When the healed scabs broke and my skin ripped open, blood flowed out again. My bent elbows were tied to my chest, then forced to straighten up the next day. The same procedure continued day after day. After a week I finally was able to bend and extend my elbows at will.

August 15. The war ends.

With no remedies available other than Mercurochrome for the wounds, Ryoko's strength gradually declined. Her hair fell out in handfuls, and her gums bled every day. Red spots appeared on her arms and thighs. It was said that when these "spots of death"

Nagasaki August 9, 1945

But it was clear I would get no treatment so I returned to school.

Around that time, Ryoko's family in Fukahori was getting the news. "Nagasaki was completely destroyed by the same new type of bomb that destroyed Hiroshima." Some were crying, thinking, "Ryoko must have been killed by the bomb!"

The names of people who were staying at the school were displayed on a sign at the school the next day. A neighbor saw the sign and told Ryoko's parents she was there.

Ryoko's father, who belonged to a fire brigade, and her uncle, who was a policeman, went to the school with a stretcher. Ryoko was taken on the stretcher to the boat and got home the night of the 10th. She was on the verge of death. She was barely conscious and couldn't speak.

We feared there might be another air attack. We took refuge in a shelter. We spread some straw mats in the shelter and rested on them. My youngest sister (then, 9) stayed with me all the time and took care of me. I was really on the brink of death.

My hair was sticking out in all directions like a bird nest. The small pieces of glass still sticking into my head were sparkling. Countless tiny pieces of glass were in my head and face. I was badly cut in 38 places. The blood running down onto my school uniform dried and made the cloth stiff. It stuck to my body. Taking that stuck cloth off my wounds was so painful I thought my skin was being torn off. My sister felt so sorry for me. She cut very carefully with scissors and took the cloth off.

She told me there was a 15-centimeter scar on my back where a big piece of glass had stabbed like a knife. She said she could see all the way down to the bone. My sister pulled as much glass out as she could,

remember most of what was happening around me. I do remember someone standing on the road yelling, "Don't sleep!" "Don't drink water!"

Along the way, Nishi was able to get a ride on the back of a strong male student. Ryoko, with glass shards piercing on her back and both arms, couldn't be held so she couldn't be carried on anyone's back.

A lady living in that neighborhood saw her armband and informed her school. Soon, two teachers pulling a cart came to pick her up. Seeing that cart, several students ran to the teachers, and the group headed for school together. Ryoko's legs were uninjured so she knelt on a straw mat in the cart, keeping her body upright making sure not to let anything press on the glass.

Coming close to the school, several more students joined the group, and all went into a classroom together. They gathered in the Etiquette Room, a tatami room where they had studied tea ceremony and flower arrangement. They spent the night there as a group. Once in a while they heard the sound of a B29. Frightened, they shrunk back against each other. All the others lay down as if they had simply fallen over, but Ryoko couldn't lie down to sleep because of the glass shards. She sat on her knees or with her feet out in front of her all night waiting for daybreak.

The next morning, since I was still bleeding badly, a teacher took me to the first-aid station in the elementary school nearby saying, "You should at least get some first aid." But when we arrived at the first-aid station, we were shocked. It was filled with people whose skin and clothes were burnt and tattered so they were nearly naked.

Thinking, "I'm better off than they are," I seemed to gain energy.

Nagasaki August 9, 1945

the buzzing sound of airplanes.

"What? Another air raid!" At the very instant I was shouting, I saw an intense flash just as a tremendous blast struck. If I had stayed on that mountain, I would have died instantly. The mountain was instantly left bald.

When the flash came, I immediately threw myself down on the concrete floor. I don't really remember what happened after that. One memory I do have is of Ueda, an older worker who called my name and helped me stand up. Her face was right in front of my eyes. I saw her again by chance a month later in a first-aid station set up in Shinkozen Elementary School. She had no obvious injury to her face or body, but I found out that she died a week later.

I was covered in blood due to the glass that the blast blew into my whole body—my arms, my back, even some in my face. I had dropped down onto my stomach so my front was protected. The glass from the skylight above me blew down and pierced my back and arms. My right elbow was ripped open. It looked like a pomegranate.

I heard that the worker sitting and writing right next to me died when a window frame hit her in the back.

I knew I had to get out. I went out the back door of the factory. I heard later that those who ran out the front entrance facing the hypocenter suffered much more from secondary exposure.

Just outside the back door was a stretch of rice fields. One of my sandals slipped off in the mud but I just kept running.

As I walked through debris that was burning hot and smoldering, I met Nishi, a classmate. She found a shoe along the way and let me wear that. The shoe belonged to a small child whose foot was half the size of mine, but I had no other choice.

Nishi appeared to be without injury, but she had to sit down frequently and throw up. All I could do was flee. I really don't

My battle with A-bomb illness continues.

Ryoko Iwanaga
Born in May 1928. Exposed to the bombing at Bunkyo-machi, 1.1 kilometers from the hypocenter. She was 17 and suffered serious injury. After lingering on the verge of death, she recovered, recuperated at home, became a nurse's assistant at a clinic, then worked for the post office and got married. She is still fighting with physical conditions officially recognized as due to the atomic bombing. At eighty-six, she resides in Nagayo-cho, Nishi Sonogi-gun, Nagasaki Prefecture.

Countless glass shards pierced my body causing hellish pain.

After graduating from Nagasaki Prefectural Girls High School, Ryoko Iwanaga was assigned to office work related to weapons manufacture. She was in the volunteer corps of the Design Section, Engineering Department II, Mitsubishi Ordnance Factory in Bunkyo-machi. Her job was to record manufacturing times per part. Her office was in the corner of a large factory building.

Her house was at Fukahori, 12 kilometers from the hypocenter. Ryoko left home early that morning, taking a ferry leaving at 6 o'clock. She arrived at Ohato Wharf after a 1-hour boat ride. From there, she took a streetcar to her office.

Soon after she arrived, at around 8:30, an air-raid warning sounded. She took refuge with fellow workers on the mountain behind the factory. When the warning was cleared, she went back to the factory.

I went back to the factory and resumed my work. Suddenly, I heard

Nagasaki August 9, 1945

experienced an atomic bombing, I am determined to continue working as hard as I can for the total abolition of nuclear weapons.

"Would you like to go to UN Headquarters, Mr. Yoshida?" I ended up being appointed delegation leader and went to the UN with three high school Peace Messengers on November 15, 1999. We visited Under Secretary General Jayantha Dhanapala and gave him 66,048 signatures on petitions calling for the elimination of nuclear weapons. The Under Secretary General told us that he was genuinely grateful for our action.

These days, the Peace Messengers sometimes deliver signatures to UN Headquarters in Geneva. I visited UN Headquarters in New York in 2005, 2008 and 2010. When we visited in 2005 we observed the NPT (Nuclear Nonproliferation Treaty) Review Conference, then met with a group of NGOs in New York.

I was deeply impressed because some said, "We don't know much about the atomic bombings of Hiroshima and Nagasaki. We want to hear directly from survivors. We want them to speak."

On May 5th that year we toured the National Museum of the USAF in Dayton, Ohio. The B29 Bockscar, which dropped the atomic bomb on Nagasaki, was displayed all polished and shiny. Thinking, "This is the one that dropped the bomb! This plane caused a lot of casualties!" I was speechless. My body shivered with anger.

The Nagasaki Peace Ceremony on August 9th, 2012, was attended by Clifton Truman Daniel, grandson of President Truman, the man who ordered the dropping of the atomic bombs. Clifton is promoting the abolition of nuclear weapons.

I met him by chance, and we pledged to work together to eliminate nuclear weapons. That "historic handshake" to move beyond our tragic history is an unforgettable memory.

I hold firmly in my mind the humanism and absolute pacifism contained in the Declaration Calling for the Abolition of Nuclear Weapons. That document changed my life. As a person who

My first sit-in demonstration was convened by the Citizens' Group to Protest Nuclear Testing the next Sunday in Peace Park. I have continued such activities, and my 43rd sit-in demonstration was to protest the third underground nuclear test by North Korea in 2013. I didn't mean to hide my activities from my family, but thinking that they were not important enough to mention, I kept silent. Then, during one of the sit-ins, I appeared on TV. My wife was watching the news and said, "Hey, that's my husband! What's he doing there?"

That is when my four children learned what I was doing. Now they know they are second-generation survivors of an atomic bombing, and I hope they will eventually become active. At the moment, they are not as interested as I am. I certainly expect my grandchildren to do something.

"A blank for 48 years! I turned my back on the atomic bombing for that long." This feeling grew into a great irritation, and I began thinking, "I have to fill that blank."

Then I received an invitation from a person I was with at a sit-in. "We're going to deliver petitions opposing nuclear tests to the embassies of nuclear weapon states in Tokyo. Why don't you come with us?"

I immediately decided to join that group. "Yes, please take me along."

I went to Tokyo many times delivering petitions against nuclear testing to the US and Russian embassies, other embassies, and the Japanese Ministry of Foreign Affairs.

In Nagasaki, one of our annual nuclear weapons abolition activities is the High School Students Signature Campaign. The committee that directs that campaign selects two Hiroshima Nagasaki Peace Messengers to deliver the signed petitions to UN Headquarters in New York.

deformed?" I had never told my wife about my exposure, so my anxiety just grew and grew, one sleepless night after the next.

On the day of the birth, I stood in front the delivery room praying, "Please let our baby be born normal." I was so relieved to find out that the baby had no defects. After that, I applied for an Atomic Bomb Survivor Health Book just in case something happened to my health.

We were blessed with one boy and three girls, but I was still determined. "I will never tell anyone about my exposure."

My first daughter married when I was 53. The full text of the Declaration Calling for the Abolition of Nuclear Weapons by Josei Toda was displayed on the second floor at the SGI Hall where my daughter's wedding ceremony took place. The declaration was the size of a tatami mat (about 3 x 6 feet), and I was just casually looking at it when my eyes were drawn to a certain part of the text. "Even if a country should conquer the world through the use of nuclear weapons, the conquerors must be viewed as devils, as evil incarnate." Before I knew what I was doing, I was writing the whole text in my notebook.

The Declaration concluded as follows: "I believe it is the mission of every member of the youth division in Japan to disseminate this idea throughout the globe." What if we change the words "member of the youth division" to "A-bomb survivors"? It was at that moment that I thought again about the atomic bombing experience I had concealed for 48 years, ever since I was five years old. It rose up within me, and I honestly thought, "I can't stay silent. I have to raise my voice!"

As soon as I came home, I made a phone call to City Hall and requested the phone numbers of the four survivor's organizations I had heard were in Nagasaki City. I called all of them and ended up applying for membership in the Nagasaki Atomic bomb Survivors Council because Secretary Yamada was so kind to me.

Nagasaki August 9, 1945

completed junior high on Battle Ship Island and got a live-in job at a bakery in Nagasaki City.

His job was to operate a machine that cut bread dough, loaf by loaf. After 3 months he pushed some dough into the machine with his finger extended too far into the machine. He suffered a serious injury that took part of his left index finger.

He was moved to the cake section and worked there for a while. Then he heard from his grandmother that his father had wanted to open a café until the day he died. Isao wanted to do the same.

He started to work for a café in Nagasaki and went to Tokyo to study the café business. Starting at a coffee stand at Takashimaya Department Store, he studied coffee for three years in Tokyo. He had promised his grandmother he would go back to Nagasaki after three years, so he went back to Nagasaki, but there was no job for him. He worked several places, including a Chinese noodle stand, and finally got a job at a Chinese restaurant. There he trained himself as a cook and later opened his own restaurant.

On becoming independent, a relative introduced him to a young woman arranged to be his marriage partner. He was very busy because he had just opened his restaurant but he went on two dates with her. First, he rode a motorbike to see her at her house in Sasebo. Then, they met to talk in a café in front of the railway station. The third time he met her was at their wedding ceremony at her parents' house in Shimabara. Because he had decided he had no relationship whatsoever to the atomic bombing, he didn't tell her about his exposure, even after she became his wife.

I will never forget that when she was about to deliver our first son, all of a sudden, I was filled with anxiety. I remembered that I had been exposed to the atomic bombing so I thought, "What if the baby's

drive me crazy. In Nagasaki when I was younger and in Gamagori, this caused me to get bullied in schools. They called me "Scab Boy!"

That bullying was one reason I decided to be rid of my A-bomb experience. By "get rid" I didn't mean, "I won't talk about it." I simply decided the whole thing had nothing to do with me. Once I cut my relationship to the atomic bombing, I had no problem seeing TV reports or newspaper articles regarding the August 9 ceremony. I was not just enduring the pain. I actually made it go away. The bombing was something that had nothing to do with me. I believe this was partly made possible by not living in Nagasaki from the 2nd grade of elementary school until the 2nd year in junior high school. I was living with my aunt in Aichi Prefecture when I convinced myself that "my A-bomb exposure went away during those six years."

I don't remember if it was candy or sweet cake, but I remember wanting something sweet. I took some money from my foster father's wallet to buy some sweets. He knew I stole his money, but he didn't say anything.

His kindness was hard on me. It made me decide to work so I could buy what I wanted with my own money. When I was a 1st year student in junior high school, I started delivering newspapers. I was very happy when I bought the rain boots I wanted so much with my first paycheck.

Just before Isao went into his 3rd year of junior high, his foster father was forced to retire, and the family fell on economic hard times. Isao was sent to live with another of his father's sisters. Their house was on Battle Ship Island in Nagasaki Prefecture. That island was a coalmine for Mitsubishi Shipbuilding and was thriving due to the post-war restoration boom. His new house was on seventh floor in high-rise building, which was quite rare at that time. Isao

fire was spreading by the minute. By the next day, it had burned a third of our neighborhood.

There were too many people in the shelter. I had nowhere to step. The smell of sweat and burns made me sick. Still, people naked from the waist up and others burnt and blistered all over were carried in on wooden doors one after the next. I remember round slices of cucumber being placed on red skin. They used cucumbers as an emergency treatment for burns because that was all they had.

We stayed in the shelter one night and returned home the next day. Our house and the houses in our immediate area escaped the fire. I continued to live with my grandmother and entered Nita Elementary School a year and a half later.

Soon after Isao entered elementary school, his grandmother fell ill. The following year, he was sent to his father's eldest sister's house in Gamagori, Aichi Prefecture. Isao lived there from second grade to his second year in junior high school. His aunt and her husband had no child of their own, and they took loving care of Isao. But having moved to a completely new place, he developed the strong feeling that he was all alone. He felt he would have to live his life by himself.

Disorders due to radiation were generally called "A-bomb disease," and two of the 11 certified disorders were applicable to me. One is Spondylosis Deformans, an inflammation of spinal joints. Mine gets worse every year.

Another is reduced white blood cell count. My main symptom is scabs all over my body. A crop of pimples or sores develops somewhere on my body, on my head, face, chest, back and so on. They suppurate and ooze pus, then produce scabs. The pain and itchiness

entered the backdoor with the wash, the world outside of our window was brilliantly illuminated by a bright light. I didn't hear anything like an explosion, but a strong wind shook the sliding paper doors causing the house to rattle.

I stood still for a while. For some reason, I started to worry about my desk. I went upstairs and found the window glass shattered. A chest and bookcase had fallen over. My room was enveloped in thick smoke that was swirling up as if somebody had turned over a charcoal grill.

"Let's run for the shelter," Grandma said to me in a daze. I left the house holding my grandmother's hand. The sky was cloudy and dark, like twilight. I learned later that the atomic cloud had covered the whole sky blocking the sunlight.

On our way through the dim light to the air-raid shelter located halfway up a hill about 40 to 50 meters from our house, I couldn't think of anything but my thirst.

"I want some water! Give me water!" I said. A soldier came across and gave me his canteen. I can still remember how delicious that water was.

We made our way pushing aside debris from fallen houses. I saw a galvanized sheet swinging and about to fall from the roof of a collapsed house. Suddenly, that sheet dropped and fell right toward me all. I escaped a direct hit but the edge scratched my mouth, making a deep cut 2.5 centimeters long. Blood gushed out.

My grandmother handed me the cotton towel that had been covering her head. I pushed it down on my cut crying, "It hurts! It hurts!" We finally reached the shelter. I still carry the scar from that cut.

When I turned back and looked out from the entrance to the shelter, I saw red flames rising up all around the railway station. The

Nagasaki August 9, 1945

We delivered over 66,000 signatures demanding the abolition of nuclear weapons to the UN.

Isao Yoshida

Born August 1940. At four, he was exposed to the atomic bombing in his house at Naka-shin-machi, 3.9 kilometers from the hypocenter. After graduating from junior high school, he worked in restaurants and a café to learn the skills, then opened a Chinese restaurant of his own. He married and had a son and three daughters. He had never told anyone about his A-bomb experience until, after reading the "Declaration Calling for the Abolition of Nuclear Weapons," he decided, "I can't be quiet. I have to raise my voice!" He joined a survivors association and worked for the movement to abolish nuclear weapons. At 74, he resides in Koga-machi, Nagasaki City.

The Turning Point: "Declaration Calling for the Abolition of Nuclear Weapons"

Isao Yoshida was the second son of parents who managed a china shop. His father died young; his older brother died when Isao was two. His mother was in her mid-twenties and, taking his grandmother's advice, remarried. Isao went to live with his grandmother. Three years later, 15 days before Isao turned five.

I was at home at Naka-shin-machi near Hollander Slope, 3.9 kilometers from the hypocenter. My grandmother was doing her wash at a community well. I was playing next to her when she suddenly shouted, "Enemy planes! Get in the house!"

Rushing in through our backdoor I turned and glanced back up at the sky. I remember the shiny American plane. Just as my grandmother

CONTENTS

In Commemoration 4

Isao Yoshida 8
Ryoko Iwanaga 17
Tsugiya Umebayashi 25
Yasuko Nakao 33
Masahiro Tanigawa 42
Nobuharu Takahira 48
Yuriyo Hama 55
Mitsuko Iwamoto 62
Fusae Fukushita 70
Masaki Morimoto 76
Yasuko Tasaki 82
Teruko Yamaguchi 89
Kwon Sun Gun 96
Hiroshi Baba 103

Reading Eyewitness Testimonies 1 112
Reading Eyewitness Testimonies 2 115

This time we publish this atomic bomb story collection in Japanese and English. This is a good chance to send the "real voice of survivors." We would be most grateful if we are able to share our mission and responsibility to pass on "the spirit of Nagasaki" to future generations accurately.

April 2015

Teruhiko Yoshioka
Chairman
Nagasaki Peace Committee

deeply. I was profoundly shaken by the survivors' desire to protect others. They are not moved by hatred or grief. They want to help us. I became all the more convinced that we have to pass the wisdom as well as the A-bomb testimonies of the survivors to future generations.

Several members of our group obtained testimony from their parents or grandparents, hearing their stories for the first time. Some were almost traumatized themselves by the raw recollections. The survivors didn't want to tell their closest loved ones because they wanted to protect them. But then, to protect all of us, they decided to talk.

Looking at their faces we don't see or feel in daily life the deep sorrow they have known. In listening to their stories, I have felt great anger, but I have never felt that coming from the survivors.

We interviewed many atomic bomb witnesses and compiled their stories in "First-hand stories of Nagasaki – Cries for Peace from High School Students" (published August 1976 by Daisanbunmei-sha). Most of them are deceased now. Among those who contributed to this book are entry survivors, in-utero survivors or Korean residents of Japan. Their backgrounds vary, but all of them said something to the effect of, "Maybe this will be my last chance to contribute." They all shared openly their valuable experiences.

The 70th anniversary of the war and the atomic bombings should not end as a memorable event. This anniversary should not be a milestone. It should be a new start, a point of departure or a leap forward toward a powerful people's movement to heed the cries of the atomic bomb survivors. We look around the world today and still see 16,000 nuclear warheads. We must never allow the use of a single one. Nuclear weapons and human beings can never coexist. It is our Nagasaki Peace Committee's mission to raise the sense of "Nuclear weapons as the embodiment of absolute evil" in world spiritual level.

In Commemoration

This summer will mark the 70th anniversary of the atomic bombing of Nagasaki. I heard on the news that the average age of the atomic bomb survivors is close to 80, and those who possess an Atomic Bomb Survivor Health Book now number less than 200,000 nationwide. Japanese born after WWII now account for 80 percent of our population. Inevitably the memories of war and the atomic bombings are fading, but the voices calling for preservation of those memories have been around a long time and are getting stronger.

I am a second-generation survivor. I contacted some friends, and, after some discussion, we formed "The Society to Hand Down Nagasaki Stories." This happened when I was a high school student about 40 years ago. I wanted to hear about the bombing and tell the stories I heard to as many people as possible. I tried once 30 years after the bombing. I walked door to door, but I found the project much more difficult than I had expected.

A-bomb survivors are reluctant to speak. To tell the story of the atomic bombing is to recall and even relive memories the survivors would prefer to conceal and forget. Remembering is more than recalling grotesque sights. It's reviving memories like the "smell of death" that penetrated and stayed for a long time deep inside noses. Even so, I kept expressing my earnest desire to preserve the memories, some decided to speak.

In the process of persuading the survivors, one response I encountered repeatedly and will never forget. "Since you are young, you need to learning about the bombing, and I guess I have to tell you. No one else should ever suffer what we did." These words touched me

Nagasaki
August 9, 1945
Telling the Story of Nagasaki Seventy Summers Later

DAISANBUNMEI-SHA
TOKYO